THE FICTION LAB

COLLECTION OF TWENTY SHORT STORIES

ASHIA WADEHRA

To everyone who's ever scribbled a story in the margins of
their notebook,
daydreamed in class, or stayed up too late chasing an
idea—
this book is for you.

May these pages remind you that your voice matters,
your imagination has power,
and your stories deserve to be heard.

Keep writing. Keep dreaming.
The world is listening.

Contents

Preface

Hi there,

If you're holding this book, thank you. That already means more than you know.

This collection of stories was written one page at a time, often late at night, between school assignments, weekend hangouts, and moments of self-doubt. These stories come from the jumble of thoughts, emotions, and dreams that fill the in-between spaces of our lives.

Each story is only a few pages long, but inside those pages are characters who felt real to me, questions I didn't know how to answer, and ideas I just had to get out of my head and into the world. Some stories are light and fun, others are a bit messy or strange, and a few might hit closer to home than expected.

These stories are short, but they come from a big place: a growing heart, an overthinking mind, and a love for storytelling.

Enjoy

Acknowledgements

Writing this book has been a wild, exciting, and sometimes overwhelming ride—and I definitely didn't do it alone.

First, thank you to my family, for letting me turn the house into a creative chaos zone, for reading early drafts (even when they didn't fully make sense), and for always encouraging me to keep writing, even when I wanted to delete everything and start over.

To my friends—thank you for being my sounding board and idea testers. Your support, inside jokes, and honesty meant the world.

A huge thanks to every teacher who ever encouraged my writing, told me to keep going, or gave me the space to be creative. You planted seeds I didn't even realize were growing.

To every author, artist, and storyteller who inspired me—thank you for showing me what stories can do. Your words made me want to find my own.

And finally, to every reader flipping through these pages: thank you. I wrote these stories hoping someone like you might find them and feel something real. If you did, then it was all worth it.

ONE

BEYOND THE MANSION'S SHADOWS

The darkness gathered around us as we stood before the Ravenswood Mansion, its decaying pillars and towers seeming to whisper eerie tales of the past. I exchanged a nervous glance with Liam, his face had an expression full of excitement but he was just as worried as me. We knew we had to explore this haunted house someday, we just didn't expect that day to be today.

You're probably wondering what I'm talking about, so let me fill you in. Liam is my older brother; he's the middle kid in our family. And there's a rumor that our neighboring house is haunted. This rumor has lasted for years, almost our entire lives. At first, we would never believe it because nothing queer really happened. But soon, people would move into the house and only a couple days later... they would randomly leave. Then the house was on sale for a long time, until another couple bought it. They left too and told us that it truly was haunted with evil spirits.

The worst part was when a family of 5 just like us, moved in. Who in the right mind would rent a house said to be haunted when you have 3 kids?! We would barely be able to get any sleep at night because there were so many screams coming from that house every night. Me and Liam would go to our parent's room every night and somehow, they were always fast asleep. That always left us with only one option left, annoy the oldest sibling; which in our case is Charlie.

Charlie would tell us to chill but by seeing the look on his face, we knew that even he wasn't chill. Every night, me and Liam would talk about how one day we were going to explore the creepy mansion when nobody lived there and it wasn't on sale. Every time we brought up the topic, Charlie would tell us to cut it out because, being the protective brother that he is, he wouldn't let us take that risk.

Anyways, fast-forward to what's happening right now. Me and Liam approach the mansion. We look at each other with a doubtful look on our face thinking if we should actually go through with the plan. Neither of us can take the pressure so Liam asks, "Why is this place called Ravenswood Mansion, anyways?" I tell him that it was the name of the first owner of this house- Mary Ravenswood and people say that her ghost haunts those who dare to step foot in her house.

Then I tease him by saying, "Wow, your little sister knows more than you." Liam tells me to think about the situation we're in right now instead of acting funny and stupid. For once, I take him seriously and take a step back out of fear. We had only one decision to make, "should we go in or not?" and that is a very difficult question.

The windows are dark and filled with shadows that play tricks on your eyes. We can already see the dust, cobwebs, creaking doors, cockroaches, mist, shadows and ripped curtains. The towers look as if they're skeletal fingers stretching towards the moon.

Cracked bricks and peeling paint revealed the house's long neglect, while overgrown vines clawed at the walls. The windows, dark and empty, seemed to reflect the shadows lurking within, rather than the moonlight outside. A chilling wind whistled through broken panes and creaking shutters, carrying whispers of the past. The overgrown yard was a tangled mess of twisted branches and decaying leaves, as if nature itself was repelled by the house's presence.

The air was thick with the scent of dust, a testament to years of disuse. A cold draft snaked through the broken windows, carrying with it the scent of decay and something else, something indefinable and unsettling. The silence was broken only by the creaks and groans of the old house, and the occasional whisper carried on the wind. The walls seemed to whisper secrets, and the floorboards groaned under the weight of unseen presences. A chill ran down my spine, not from the cold, but from the sense of unease present in the air.

It was horrifying, the house looked abandoned and lifeless. A sudden drop in temperature, a chilling breeze from nowhere, and the feeling of being watched... it made me regret my decision. Just as we were walking closer towards the mansion, I tripped on a weed and scratched my knee. It was bleeding a lot, I couldn't see much in the dark but somebody (not Liam) picked me up and patted the dirt off of my shirt. I tried to see who it was. I rubbed my eyes and turned on my flashlight. It was Charlie, turns out he knew that we came here tonight.

Charlie said, "Are you guys crazy? Whose idea was it to come here?" Liam pointed at me without hesitation. This made Charlie lose his temper so much that he screamed at me, "Wow Leena. Stay in your limits for once, this is one thing that I just don't trust you to take upon yourself." The fact that he said it really loudly in the middle of the night. He tells us that we had to go back home. I'm 13 years old and I'm not scared of anything in particular so honestly, I think that I'm capable of going in there by myself. While Charlie drags us back home, Liam tries to start a conversation with me. Obviously, I ignore him because he should know not to joke around me when I'm mad at him. The worst part- he doesn't even think I have any right to be mad at him for telling Charlie that it was my idea to sneak out and go to a haunted house.

The second we reach home, I barge into my room, throw my bag pack and flashlight on bed, and slam the door on my brothers' faces as hard as possible. Charlie just walks into my room and says, "Leena Fernandes, I'm 18 and you're 13. Don't try and act smart. Your mind tricks don't work on me." I try to hold my smile until he goes back to his own room. I start laughing the second he leaves. I'm pretty smart, that's why he said 'mind' tricks. But the line, "your mind tricks don't work on me" is actually a line from Star Wars 1- The Phantom Menace. Watto is a Toydarian scoundrel who runs a junkyard on Tatooine, he says this to Jedi Qui-Gon-Jinn. My siblings and I love Star Wars, so it was cool to see Charlie say the line in real life.

Liam walks into the room and says, "Hey Leena, I'm sorry for ratting you out like that." I tell him, "Its ok but have you ever noticed how persistent Charlie is about us never going into the Ravenswood mansion? Its honestly weird. Don't you think so?" Liam agrees with me. I have a better idea. We take out a notebook in which we write down our plan.

Step 1: pretend to eat an expired yogurt, fake being sick.

Step 2: wait till Charlie goes to school, and mom and dad leave for work.

Step 3: sneak out and explore the mansion once and for all.

Step 4: reach back home after solving the mystery and confronting who's behind it.

That was our plan. It wasn't a bad idea but we still need to figure out some of this on the spot. We don't know what we could find in there but I guess we'll have to face it when the time comes.

So, we walk to Charlie's room and say that we're hungry. He says that we can eat something that we have in the kitchen or can make ourselves a sandwich. He suspects that we might go to the mansion again so he comes outside to the kitchen with us.

Liam asks, "Can I have this yogurt that I found in the fridge?" Charlie says ok without caring so to grab his attention Liam says,

"Hey Leena, want to share this yogurt with me, that I found in the fridge?"

"Oh sure. But looks like its expired."

"But its in the 2-week buffer zone."

"Great. Cause Charlie always says its ok to eat expired food if it's in the buffer zone."

"Let me just grab us some spoons then."

Of course, it wasn't actually expired. We wouldn't risk getting food poisoning. So, we ate it and went to bed after that. Turns out, neither of us could fall asleep. We ended up grabbing our i-pad and laptop to play some video games and watch movies.

Next morning, we get out of bed and go downstairs. I tell Charlie and my parents that my stomach hurts and I can't go to school. My mom says, "Honey, you fake being sick too many times. By now, we know you're not actually sick." Luckily, Liam backs me up by saying, "Mom, its not a joke. Even my stomachs hurting so much. I think we have food poisoning."

We giggled as we pretended to be sick, clutching our stomachs and making grossed-out faces. Mom was worried, but she eventually fell for it, keeping us home from school while she and Dad headed to the office. Charlie, our older brother, was already at school, oblivious to our plan.

As soon as the front door closed, we high-fived each other. "Yes! We did it, Liam!" I exclaimed. My brother grinned, and we quickly got dressed in our exploration gear. We snuck out of the house, making our way to the infamous Ravenswood Mansion.

The creepy old house loomed before us, its tall spires and turrets reaching toward the sky like skeletal fingers as always. We approached cautiously, our hearts racing with excitement and a touch of fear. We had been trying to explore this place for weeks, but Charlie always seemed to find out and stop us.

As we stepped inside, the creaking floorboards beneath our feet seemed to echo through the empty halls. We called out, "Hello?" but only silence replied. We began to explore, room by room, searching for signs of the ghostly Mary Ravenswood.

In the attic, we stumbled upon an old trunk, adorned with dusty locks and faded labels. Liam's eyes lit up. "Leena, look!" he whispered, as we carefully opened the trunk. Inside, we found a collection of old photographs and a diary belonging to our parents.

As we flipped through the pages, a picture caught my eye. It was an old black-and-white photo of a girl with a kind smile and piercing green eyes. The caption read, "Mary Ravenswood, age 6." Suddenly, a chill ran down my spine.

Liam noticed my expression and followed my gaze to the photo. "Who's that?" he asked, his voice barely above a whisper. I shook my head, feeling a strange connection to the girl in the picture.

As we continued to explore, strange occurrences began to happen. Doors creaked open on their own, and faint whispers seemed to follow us. It was as if Mary Ravenswood was trying to communicate with us.

And then, we stumbled upon a hidden room deep within the mansion. Inside, we found a series of old photographs, articles and a birth certificate with our family name. The article mentioned a tragic accident involving a young girl named Mary Ravenswood, who was our older sister

We exchanged shocked glances. "Mary Ravenswood is our sister?" Liam asked, his voice trembling. I nodded, feeling tears well up in my eyes. We had never known about her, and our parents had kept it a secret all these years.

As we stood there, frozen in shock, the whispers grew louder, and the air seemed to vibrate with an otherworldly energy. Suddenly, a figure materialized before us – a gentle, ethereal presence with piercing green eyes.

"Mary?" I whispered, my voice barely audible. The ghostly figure nodded, a soft smile on her face. "I'm glad you came," she said, her voice like a gentle breeze. "I've been waiting for you, Leena and Liam."

As we gazed at our long-lost sister, the mystery of the haunted mansion began to unravel. But new questions arose – questions about our family's past, about Mary's life and death, and about the secrets our parents had kept hidden for so long.

We asked what happened. All she said was, "Don't worry about me. Let the past be the past. I'll always remember you guys and stay by your sides. I may not be there physically but I'm there in spirit. Talk to mom and dad, you'll get answers. I love you, always have and always will. Good luck." She chuckled as she went back to the afterlife or wherever she was all this time.

We demanded questions from our parents as soon as they got home. They always told us that it was just a coincidence our last name was Ravenswood and that we could never be related to the ghost next-door.

Our parents told us that she was Charlie's twin sister. When they were little kids, them and our driver got into an accident. The driver was fine and so was Mary. But Charlie...not so much.

He was in terrible condition, covered in blood and bruises, in a coma for days. The doctors said that there was barely any chance he could make it, he needed a heart transplant. The only way he would live was if there was a willing donor, there were quite a few but none of them had the blood group AB+.

When everyone had lost hope, Mary walked forward with tears in her eyes and said, "Mom, Dad. I'm already diagnosed with cancer; it will kill me one day. Mine and Charlie's DNA and blood group are the exact same, I'm willing to give him my heart. I don't want you to lose both of your kids."

After that day, we didn't question our parents. We also visited Mary as much as we could.

We didn't doubt it because it seemed like a believable story. But this led to the uprising of more questions in my head. What else could our parents have been hiding from us.

They said that they didn't tell us about this to protect us. We would have been completely fine even if we knew about it. This wasn't a situation in which we needed protection, it was as if they just lied to us our whole lives.

I talked to Liam about these thoughts in my head. But he brushed it off saying that it was a one-time thing. He also mentioned that if our parents told us about this horrifying mystery when we were just innocent kids, we would have freaked out and eventually gotten addicted to Mary.

I guess now I understand how it could affect our lives because little children go around telling their family secrets. And if we're affected and shocked by this truth now, it would have been way worse back then.

Our parents know what they're doing. I couldn't possibly imagine how I would have reacted if they told me that when I was 2 years old. They made a decision for the best. Now its time to get back to my not so ordinary life.

TWO

COLD HANDS, BRAVE HEART

Everyone in the world has a superpower. Everyone.

Some can fly, some can shapeshift, some can shoot fire from their hands or talk to animals or heal with a single touch. It's like a universal lottery where every single person got something incredible. And me? I got ice.

I can freeze things. Control ice, make it form out of thin air, lower the temperature of a room, even create snow if I focus really hard. Sounds cool, right? It's not.

Not when you're me—a walking accident, an unwanted sidekick, and the punchline to every joke at my school.

It's funny how people think that just having powers makes you special. That it gives your life meaning. But for me, my power has been nothing but a curse.

It started when I was around nine—our garden fountain froze solid on a summer day. My mom thought it was a weird plumbing issue. By ten, I had turned my entire bathroom into a frozen cave because I sneezed too hard. By twelve, I was already being called names at school— "Daisy the Disaster", "Frost Freak", and my personal favourite:

"Snowflake Screw-Up."

People don't get it. My ice isn't flashy like fire. It's not useful like healing. And it's definitely not heroic like flying or super strength. It's slow. It's cold. It makes things slippery and dangerous. And when I try to help, I always make things worse.

I remember the day that sealed my reputation forever. The day everything fell apart.

There was a monster—some mutant lizard thing, the size of a city bus, stomping through town. Everyone who had even a hint of a useful power rushed out to fight it. Kids in my grade were throwing fireballs, creating barriers, flying above buildings and attacking from the air. It was like a superhero flash mob, and I just... stood there, unsure.

But I wanted to help. I really did.

So, I thought: "Hey, maybe I can help stop the thing. Maybe if I make the ground icy, it'll slip and fall and everyone will cheer. I imagined the news headlines: 'Local Girl Saves the Day with Brilliant Ice Move!'"

Instead? The monster didn't slip. My friends did.

One by one, they skidded across the ice I made, tumbling, crashing into each other like some kind of slapstick comedy. One kid broke his wrist. Another chipped her tooth. And the monster got away.

To this day, people still bring it up. In the halls. In group chats. During gym class. "Hey Daisy, want to help with the basketball game? You could ice the court and knock out the team for us!" That whole scene was followed by laughter.

It was the day I learned I wasn't a hero. I was a mistake. An embarrassing footnote in other people's victories.

So now, I stay away. I don't join the city fights. I don't show off. I try not to even use my powers. I keep them locked up inside like a secret I'm ashamed of. Most days, I come home, go to my room, and just pretend to be normal.

And one day, I couldn't hold it in anymore. I cried. Not the cute, cinematic kind of crying. The real, raw, ugly kind. The kind where your chest feels like it might shatter, and the sound of your sobs bounces off your walls louder than you expect.

That's when Sam walked in.

Sam is my older brother. He's eighteen and basically everything I'm not. Confident. Funny. Popular. And of course, his power is super speed. The guy's a blur—literally. He's part of the City Patrol, helps with emergency rescues, has a patch on his uniform and everything. People look at him and see a real hero.

I didn't hear him knock. I was curled up on my bed, hugging my pillow like it could keep me from falling apart, when I felt him sit beside me.

"Hey," he said gently. "What's going on?"

I didn't want to tell him. Not at first. But something about the way he sat there—quiet, patient, real—made me talk. I told him everything. About how I felt useless. About the teasing. The monster incident. The ice. The embarrassment. I told him I felt like the worst superhero ever.

He didn't laugh. He didn't pity me. He listened.

And when I was done, he said something I'll never forget.

"You just haven't found the right fight yet, Daisy. Ice isn't useless. You're not useless. You're just different. And that's okay."

I looked at him through red, puffy eyes. "What difference does it make if I only ever mess things up?"

"Then let's fix that. Come with me."

That's when he told me about a villain. A guy named Scorch—real name unknown. He had laser eyes, could fly, and left entire buildings melted behind him. But he had one weakness: he could only fly and shoot lasers when he wasn't injured. The moment he took damage, even a small cut, his powers shut down temporarily.

Sam said he was going to stop him. And he wanted me to help.

"Why?" I asked, still stunned.

"Because I need someone who can land that first hit," he said. "And I believe in you."

I was terrified. My hands were shaking as we approached the hideout Scorch had taken over. The air smelled like burning metal. Sirens were wailing in the distance. Sam ran ahead to draw his attention, zipping back and forth to dodge the lasers.

I stayed hidden behind a car, breathing fast, trying to calm the storm in my chest.

"You'll mess it up again", that ugly voice in my head said. "They'll all fall. The monster will escape. You're not a hero."

But then I remembered Sam's voice. "I believe in you."

I closed my eyes. Focused. Felt the cold rise in my veins like it always did. I formed an icicle, long and sharp, and held it like a javelin.

When Sam gave me the signal—just a flash of his hand—I stepped out, took a deep breath, and threw.

The icicle spun through the air, shimmering. And it hit. Right in Scorch's arm.

He screamed. Blood spurted. And in that moment, his powers stopped. No more lasers. No more flying.

Sam zipped in, tackled him to the ground, and slapped the anti-power cuffs on his wrists. I stood there, heart pounding, watching as the hero teams arrived and took him away.

We even made sure he got treated at the hospital. Because that's what heroes do.

Afterwards, Sam clapped a hand on my shoulder. "You did amazing, Daisy. I couldn't have done that without you."

I cried again. But this time, they were the good kind of tears.

Since then, I've started training more. Finding ways to use my ice in smarter, more helpful ways. I've made frozen bridges to rescue stranded people. I've used cold fog to blind getaway drivers. I've even made protective shields during a fire to keep people from getting burned.

It's still hard. People still remember the old Daisy. But I'm starting to change the story.

All thanks to my brother. Because sometimes, you don't need to change who you are.

Sometimes... you just need the right influence by the right person. And that's all the help you need.

THREE

LIGHTS, CAMERA, CONTENT

If you had told me a year ago that I'd have a fanbase, a manager, and people analysing my outfit choices, I probably would've laughed with a mouth full of popcorn and told you I was too boring for all that. I wasn't the loud one in the group, or the artsy one, or the one with a "vibe." I was just... Candice. The girl who loved movie marathons, spent too much time arranging Spotify playlists, and had a weird obsession with Lego.

It all started on a random Saturday. My friends and I were at Maya's place, lounging around and doing what we usually do: absolutely nothing productive. Someone suggested we try a trending dance challenge—it was all over the internet. We weren't trying to be perfect. In fact, the whole appeal was how terribly we executed it. I wore mismatched socks, no makeup, and a ratty hoodie with a faded graphic of F.R.I.E.N.D.S. on it. Maya's little brother recorded it on his phone. I almost told him not to post it, but I was too lazy to care.

That video changed everything.

The video was posted to Maya's Instagram stories and later her profile. We forgot about it within ten minutes. But two days later, Maya called me in the middle of my lunch break, practically screaming into the phone.

"Candice. You need to look at this. NOW."

I thought it was another dumb meme or a group chat scandal. Instead, I saw that our video had been shared on a popular meme page. It had over a million views, and the top comment read: "That girl in the hoodie is a whole mood. Someone find her."

Guess who the girl in the hoodie was?

Suddenly, my notifications exploded. People started following my private Instagram. I had to switch it to public because requests were flooding in by the hundreds. And then—strangers started tagging me in reposts. I became a meme. A whole thread popped up: "Candice-core." Whatever that meant.

At first, I laughed. Then I panicked. Then I started replying to comments. And then—I leaned into it.

After a week of buzz, people started asking: "Do you have a YouTube channel?" I didn't, but the idea lodged in my brain like a catchy tune. I already spent hours watching video essays and blooper reels; why not create my own?

So, I made one.

My first video was a low-effort, slightly chaotic "Get to Know Me" intro. I used my phone, natural light, and edited it using a free app on my laptop. I talked about how weird it was to go viral, my favourite movies, and why I think the release of the Harry Potter movies made the books underrated. The next morning, it had 20,000 views.

I felt like I had swallowed a firework.

From there, I started posting every week. Then twice a week. I made videos where I reacted to classic movie trailers, analysed character arcs from 2000s teen dramas, and did "day in the life" vlogs. People liked that I was just being me. Unfiltered. Awkward. A little bit messy.

And somewhere along the line, I became a content creator.

Instagram became my second home. I posted goofy behind-the-scenes clips, mood boards inspired by different fictional characters, and outfit recreations from TV shows. People especially loved my "Iconic Movie Lines" edits—fast-paced, and bringing back nostalgia.

I started gaining followers. Not dozens, not hundreds—but thousands. Blue-check influencers began following me. One even messaged me about a possible collab. My heart actually stopped for a second when I saw their name pop up.

But the weirdest moment? A costume designer from one of my favourite shows DMed me saying she loved how I styled my outfits and asked if I wanted to visit the set next season.

I think I screamed.

Going viral is fun until it's not.

People expect you to be on all the time. I'd get messages like, "When's your next upload?" or "You've been quiet lately. Everything okay?" I felt like I couldn't disappear for a day without someone assuming I'd quit, died, or moved to a different planet.

I also had to deal with trolls. One of my edits went viral for the wrong reasons. A few people mocked my voice in a reaction video. Others accused me of "ruining nostalgia." I cried in the shower that night. It felt like someone had thrown dirt on something I created with love.

But every time I thought of quitting, I'd get a comment from a teenage girl saying my video helped her through a rough week. Or a DM from a guy who said he'd never seen anyone explain a show like that before. And I realized—this was bigger than just me.

Fast forward eight months: I now have a solid routine. I treat content creation like a job, but one I still genuinely enjoy. I storyboard my videos, plan my uploads, and keep a notebook filled with future edit ideas.

I still hang out with Maya and the crew. We laugh about how it all started with that cringey dance. They keep me grounded, reminding me that I'm still Candice—just Candice with a fanbase now.

I've even started dabbling in collaborations with indie filmmakers, helping them promote their projects through cinematic edits. The fact that my passion for storytelling and media turned into a platform still blows my mind.

But here's the thing: I never set out to be famous. I was just having fun with my friends. And somehow, being myself was the most influential thing I could've done.

Once my follower count started climbing steadily, I knew I couldn't keep this new world to myself. So, I introduced my friends on all my platforms. Maya, with her infectious laugh and endless energy, became a fan favourite, while Jake's dry humour and effortless cool made him an instant hit. I shared little clips and stories about each of them, showing off their quirks and personalities. People loved seeing our dynamic—it was like they were joining our little squad through the screen. The best part? They were all game for the crazy content ideas I kept throwing at them.

One of the most fun things we did together was participate in viral dance challenges. We nailed dances like Shake it to the Max, Passo Bem Solto, and APT with varying degrees of success—and sometimes epic failure, which only made the videos more relatable and hilarious. I loved how those dances brought us closer, and viewers loved the authenticity we brought to each step and stumble. The comments were full of encouragement and laughter, and soon, our group dance videos became some of the most popular posts on my Instagram and YouTube.

My new online popularity started to spill over into school life. When the student council elections rolled around, my friends convinced me to run. I wasn't sure if people would take me seriously—after all, I was just "that viral girl" who danced badly on the internet—but I decided to go for it anyway. I put together a campaign that focused on creativity, inclusion, and new opportunities for students to express themselves. The blend of my newfound confidence and the support of my followers gave me an edge, and before I knew it, I had won a spot on the student council.

As soon as I stepped into that role, I knew I wanted to make a real difference. The first thing I did was propose the creation of a content creation club at school—a space where anyone interested in making videos, podcasts, or edits could come together, learn, and create. The idea was met with enthusiasm from the council and the student body alike. We managed to secure a cozy room near the library and transformed it into a mini studio complete with cameras, lights, and editing software, donated by the school and a few local businesses that loved the idea.

Setting up the recording room was a dream come true. Watching students from all grades come in, nervous but excited, to experiment with content creation was incredibly rewarding. Some were shy at first, but within weeks, they were brainstorming ideas, shooting skits, and collaborating on projects that rivalled my early videos. It was like watching a whole new wave of creativity come to life right in our school halls. I felt proud knowing that what started as a viral dance had blossomed into a community where students could express themselves freely.

Balancing school, content creation, and student council duties wasn't always easy. Some days I felt stretched thin, waking up at dawn to film and staying up late to finish council proposals or edit videos. But every time I looked around that recording room, buzzing with energy and ideas, I remembered why I did it all. The support from my friends, the encouragement from strangers turned followers, and the spark of creativity in my peers made it worth every exhausting moment.

Looking back, it's wild to think how a simple dance video with friends turned into something so much bigger. Not just for me, but for the whole school. I'm no longer just Candice, the girl in the hoodie—I'm Candice, the creator, the student leader, and the person who helped build a space where everyone's voice can be heard. And honestly? I can't wait to see where this crazy journey takes us next.

FOUR

THE LOCKER ROOM LEGACY

I can barely bring myself to open my eyes on a Monday morning. But my alarm clock gives me no sympathy, its going to ring until I wake up- leaving me no choice but to get out of bed. Sometimes I wish I could just take out the batteries but then I would have to get a 10-minute-long lecture from my mom which is even worse than going to school at 7 AM. I guess school isn't that bad. We have physical education, singing, art and library class but there are just some subjects like math and science which absolutely drive me crazy.

So, I go on with my normal morning routine. I brush my teeth, wear my uniform, do my hair, eat breakfast and get to the bus stop. Its pretty annoying to follow the same routine every single day, my mom says everyone is annoyed by it but I think its just the universe trying to irritate me as much as possible.

The only good part about going to school is meeting my friends Lily, Leo and Jake. Lily and Leo are twins so whenever they get into an argument, its impossible to get them out of it. Its difficult to deal with them but when they set their minds to something it can lead to an awesome success or a horrible disaster. Jake on the other hand is an only child like me but he does have some pretty cool skills. He plays the electric guitar, aces almost all his exams and yet still finds some time to play football. He even made the school football team and is in the school math wizard team too.

Its not like the rest of us don't pay attention. We get above average scores too but we focus more on sports so we can get scholarships without having to put in too much of our brains. Now you might be thinking, "Why are a bunch of 12-year-olds already thinking about scholarships?" It's mainly because we have sharp minds and we already know what we want to do in the future, its better to work towards the thing you know you want to do than to try a million activities and turn out to be good in none of them.

Anyways, I get to school and the first lesson we have is geography. We have a pop quiz but I'm pretty good at it so I'm not stressing that much. Its pretty simple MCQs so I'm able to speed through it. Even the map is really easy but I forgot my colour pencils at home. Luckily Mrs. O'Donnel always keeps extras knowing we forget stuff sometimes. The rest of the quiz is just the capital cities which took me some time but I finish the quiz before the time limit.

Now I wonder, "What should I even do?" I look around to see whether my friends are done or not. Leo and Lily have telepathy or at least that's what they say. I think its true because both of them seem to be looking at each other after every question. I'm honestly not surprised they would try something like this, its just who they are.

I look over at Jake and he's done too. I assumed he would have finished before everyone else. Its in his genes, he comes from a long line of geniuses and multitaskers. I wait and wait and wait until the timer is finally over. Looks like mostly everyone was able to finish in time.

Next, we have P.E. (Physical Education). Mr. Davidson tells us that we can either go play football, basketball, cricket or throwball. He said that this time some of us could even race if we wanted to.

We have plenty of space in the basketball court because its empty. So, the basketball kids are going to play half court, the other half is going to be for throwball. Then we have gigantic circular grass field for football, not as large as the real ones but big enough. Its boundary is the race track for running. There is a small but manageable area near the skating rink to play cricket. The skating rink is closed for now though. That is how there is enough space for us to play so many sports at the same time.

"Hey Crystal! Want to join us? We're playing basketball. We just need one more person, I was hoping it could be you.", asks Leo. "Sure", I tell him. Leo has always been nice to me, so I can trust him with anything. Plus, it would be nice to play a friendly match.

The match goes awesome. Our team is winning. Leo, Ava and I scored most of the baskets. The other team was off to a good start until we kicked in our strategy. Our strategy is to go easy on them at the start- let them think they might win. But later, when they'll be tired, we up our game and play with all the energy we've been saving till half-time.

We're in the last few seconds of the match. The other team has 2 points more than us. Leo signals me to pass the ball to him but he's not free so I pass it to Ava. She knew what we were thinking but she wasn't capable enough of throwing a 3-pointer yet, by that time, even I wasn't free so she couldn't pass it back to me. Leo screams, "Ava, don't aim for the basket! Just throw the ball towards the free-throw line! I have a plan!" The second Ava throws it, Mike comes in and passes it to Leo. Leo shoots, the ball bounces on the ring three times and eventually, it goes in.

We won the match. Sometimes I think we're a little too competitive but we need that spirit. The bell rings and everyone goes back to class. Its break now so I decide to go refill my bottle but I can't find it anywhere. Lily tells me that she can't find her jacket either and that we might have left our things at the basketball court. So, we go back to look for our stuff.

Lily finds her jacket on one of the seats. But I still can't find my bottle, we looked everywhere. Lily says, "You're captain of the girls basketball team and your bottle is customized with your name on it. Maybe Mr. Davidson noticed it lying around and kept it your locker or the locker room." I'm shocked by how she just came up with that idea I tell Lily, "Wow. Looks like you've got some pretty cool detective skills."

I go check my locker and I find my bottle there. There's a lot of silence and if you know our locker rooms, there is always something or someone making noise. But it was never this quiet. I also sensed something was off, the locker room wasn't the same. Lily reassured me that it was nothing. I told her that it just felt empty. I didn't know how to describe what I was feeling but I've been in here more than a hundred times so I can easily notice when something has changed.

Lily told me, "Maybe it just feels empty because Maya left the school and they removed her locker. It'll feel weird for a while because her locker was right next to yours. I'm telling you Crystal, everything's fine." But when she said that, it made me turn around and notice that Maya's locker wasn't there anymore.

I told her, "The school never removes the locker when someone leaves the school or gets kicked off the team or anything. They just replace the name-tag and assign the locker to someone else. And I know they're not reorganizing the locker rooms because both the boys and girls teams' captains are informed. So, I would have been told that they're doing something."

I calm myself down a little but then I look carefully at the wall where Maya's locker used to be. Its really dusty, just as I'm wiping off the dust, I come across a black button. The button read, "PRESS ME!" Lily told me to leave it and just get back to class but my curiosity took over and I pressed it. The wall made a small gap on the side, it was like a sliding door. I opened the door and saw a small staircase, I went inside but it was too dark. All I could see was the exact same button on the inside, I think it was to open and close it from the inside and outside.

Before I could explore anything else or go further inside, the bell rings. It ruins the sense of mystery for me and I'm a person who loves solving mysteries. Lily was also triggered by then, she said, "we need to tell Leo and Jake about this." I completely agreed with her but we wouldn't have time to find out more throughout the day.

So, I tell her, "Me and Leo are the basketball team captains, so we have access to this place anytime throughout the whole day. I can bring in you as a +1 and Leo can bring in Jake as a +1. We have to find out what this is." We go back to class but this passageway is the only thing I can think about right now.

I wonder what could the staircase could even lead to. Let's call it the secret passageway. But the thing is no one else can find out about it. Its math class and let's just say I cannot get my mind off of the passageway so it was really difficult to even try to pay attention.

Ms. Kelly says, "Crystal. Crystal. Crystal!" she had to say my name 3 times before I knew what was happening around me.

"What is the answer to question 3?", she asked.

"Uhh, is it exercise A or B?"

"It's exercise C, question 3, part iv. Crystal, we completed A and B long back."

"24 I think"

"Oh, you're far off from the answer."

"What's the answer miss?"

"45.5 is the answer. You're not one of my brightest students but come back to your senses Crystal. You generally do much better than this. Now pay attention"

I knew I had to pay attention but it wasn't quite possible at the time. Luckily, she didn't call on me the rest of the class. I was just waiting for the bell to ring so we could have our library lesson. The day passes by so slowly. I can't wait for the day to get over but the thing is, the teachers have to stay till 5:00PM for the afternoon batch of children. So, we can't go at that time, we'll have to go back to the school at around 6:00PM.

We all go home and are waiting the whole day till 6 o'clock just so we can go to the secret passageway. I spend all day at home thinking of something to do. My mom walks into my room and says, "God Chrissy! I hate that every time I come into your room, its always dirty. Plus, you're not even doing anything. Clean your room and do your homework, don't just sit here being bored."

I have to do what my mom says unless I want a lecture. I somewhat have OCD so; I generally always keep my room clean. But this was a once in a lifetime situation, I had found a secret passageway in the middle of my school so its hard to keep my room clean. I get up to see if my room is actually that messy. "I mean how bad can it actually be?" Ok it was very dirty, I get to cleaning it. After about 10 minutes of picking up stationery, clothes, bags and laundry, its as clean as can be.

Now, onto my homework. That's going to be a little problematic because I can't exactly recall anything we learnt in class, the past entire week. I try again, and again and again but it just doesn't work. So, I give up and call Jake for some help. I tell him that I can barely focus on anything in the whole world and I just need him to send me his answers. I don't really like copying others' work and it's a thing I never do, but like I said - I couldn't focus.

After I'm done with the homework, I finally lay down on my bed to check my phone. The time was 5:30 but that works. I tell Lily, Leo and Jake to meet up at the park. I wait, sitting on a bench for some time until the rest of them arrive. We go over our plan- we enter the school as if we just felt like getting some memories before the final exams and going into the next class, but we actually go to the passageway and this time we carry flashlights too (just in case). We're going to explore each corner of that place unless it's something creepy. If it is weird and horrifying, we'll report it to the school.

We enter the school. We reach the door, just as I press the button, it becomes a sliding door again. This time even Leo and Jake are there to experience it. We walk down the staircase. It seems as if the passage was built during the school's early days- we think it was used as a maintenance tunnel or safe route during emergency situations. Over time, it was sealed off and lost to history, or at least that's what it looks like. Maybe the school was once an old mansion and this passageway was a part of its original design and structure.

We reach the end of the passage; it's like a big empty dim-lit room. The thing is it wasn't quite empty. It was filled with cobweb-covered shelves and dusty old boxes. Old yearbooks, faded photographs, handwritten journals and school magazines are scattered about. I stumble upon ancient trophies and plaques from sports teams and academic clubs that no longer even exist.

There is even an old chalkboard, which is partly divided into a pinboard. It has some strange writing on it, probably left by past students. The pinboard side is filled with pictures of students and teachers attached with red strings like it was a murder mystery movie.

As we dig deeper, we discover a school newspaper, they don't even give these out anymore. We find out the forgotten tale of a student who mysteriously disappeared and days later his body was found at sea because someone noticed blood in the water, his teacher turned out to be the one who killed him. That's why there were pictures of students and teachers, somebody was trying to figure out the murderer.

That was extremely creepy, it even gave me the heebie-jeebies and I never get the heebie-jeebies. We looked around for more about this case but what we saw was all that was left. I guess, the student took the rest of the information with them. I like mysteries, so it would have been cool to have the rest of the info too. I kept on reading what was written in the newspaper article and kept on talking about the case, not changing the subject. When I saw the scared looks on my friends' faces I decided to let go of the topic.

But that school paper was never published. So, this is basically evidence of a past hidden secret that was never recovered. The room also holds personal letters by students to the school, secret club records and even a blueprint of the school's original layout. This secret passageway was the spot where the kid trying to find the murderer of the incident came every day, I'm assuming.

This was truly an adventure, just like how one opens a time capsule years after placing it in the ground, not even remembering it was there. This was like an insight into the school's past moments and history. We decide not to inform the school about this assuming they would tear it apart and just put up an ordinary wall there and throw away all these things.

Instead, we decided to clean it up. It takes a couple of days because it was really old and dusty. We redecorate the place but don't discard any of the trophies, photographs, club records or anything. We keep all of these things and add some things of our own too.

This is a list of the new stuff we added:

- A new board which on one side is a chalkboard and on the other side a pinboard.
- A projector
- A whiteboard on the wall, with a plain white curtain on top which can be pulled down so we can watch movies or do anything online.
- 4 chairs and another table so that there are 2 people on each table.
- A tiny sofa which fits us all was the final touch of decoration.

Now, whoever is the next to discover this spot after us, this will be their spot. It will be an adventure for them just like it was for us to figure out this place. This became our new hangout spot. Now we come here every single day.

There are too many incidents we've had in that room by just 9th grade. Once, Jake didn't want to celebrate his birthday, so we decorated with balloons, got him a cake and celebrated it watching videos of us together as little kids. There's a lot of memories in that passageway. To many memories to even remember.

FIVE

THE PLAYBACK PROBLEM

I woke up on my 13th birthday expecting pancakes, balloons, maybe even a new hoodie from Mom. What I didn't expect was for her to sit at the edge of my bed, staring at me like she was about to tell me the family dog died. Spoiler: we don't even have a dog.

"Hannah," she said, in that serious voice she usually reserved for when I forgot to do the dishes, "you're officially a teenager now. Which means… the family curse begins today."

I blinked at her, still halfway tangled in my blanket. "The what begins?"

"The curse," she repeated. "Every day, from now on, you'll receive a unique, deadly curse. They can take any form. You have to deal with them yourself. No one can help you." She stood up and walked to the window like she'd just told me it might rain later. "It's tradition."

Before I could say anything, I felt a strange tingling on the back of my neck. Two glowing buttons suddenly popped into view, hovering a few inches above my head. One read

PAUSE, the other PLAY—like something from a video game. I reached up without thinking and tapped PAUSE.

The world froze. Completely. Mom stood still by the window, one hand raised mid-gesture. The birds outside stopped in mid-flight. The second hand on the wall clock hung in mid-tick. I waved my hand in front of Mom's face. Nothing. It was like everything had gone to sleep... except me.

I pressed PLAY, and the world blinked back into motion. The birds flew. The clock ticked. Mom turned around as if nothing had happened. "Well?" she said. "Any buttons yet?"

"Yeah," I mumbled. "Pause and Play."

She nodded. "Lucky. Some kids get way worse for their first curse. Your Aunt Jeanie got teleported into a cow pasture. In Scotland."

Honestly, this didn't feel like a curse at all—it felt like a power. A useful one. A cool one, even. I was still wrapping my head around it when Mom handed me a slice of toast and pointed at the clock. "Better hurry. School."

The walk to school was weird. I kept thinking about the buttons. About what would happen if I paused time and just... took a nap in the middle of the sidewalk. I didn't. But I did pause time for a few seconds when a dog started barking at me through a fence. I just wanted to see its mouth frozen mid-bark. It was hilarious.

At school, everything looked the same, but I didn't feel the same. I had this secret—this power. I wondered if anyone else was going through this too, or if I was the only cursed 13-year-old with magical buttons. I didn't even know what kind of curses would come tomorrow... or the next day. Maybe this was just Day One of something way bigger than I understood.

Still, I pushed the thought to the back of my mind. For now, time was ticking forward, and I had math class in ten minutes. Whatever this curse really was, I'd deal with it. One button press at a time.

By the time I got to second period, I had already pressed the PAUSE button three times. The first was during homeroom when Mr. Palmer wouldn't stop talking about upcoming announcements, and I swear, my brain was trying to crawl out of my ears.

I paused the day and just sat there, enjoying the perfect, golden stillness of everything around me. I studied people's frozen expressions like they were paintings. It was quiet. Peaceful. Addicting. After a few minutes of pretending to be a museum curator of time-stopped teenagers, I hit PLAY again like nothing had happened.

The second time I paused was in history class. Mrs. Beck always talked like someone was holding a grudge against her personally for being interesting. Today's topic was trade routes. I paused the day just to get up, walk around the classroom, and look at everyone's notebooks.

I saw what people were doodling, what they were writing. I even corrected a few spelling mistakes in passing. When I sat back down, I pressed PLAY, and class resumed like nothing happened. No one noticed. I felt like a ghost with God-level editing powers.

I used the third pause just before lunch, when I forgot my homework in my locker. Instead of running across the school like a maniac, I calmly paused time, strolled through the halls without anyone around, grabbed my paper, and strolled back like it was a spring afternoon.

I passed by the principal mid-sentence, her face frozen in some bizarre expression, probably scolding someone. It was honestly hilarious.

At lunch, I paused it again—fourth time—because I didn't want to wait in line for the pizza. I stepped in front of everyone, carefully moved trays and arms, grabbed the biggest slice, then returned to my spot. PLAY. Nobody said a word.

A few people looked confused, but no one had the faintest clue what I'd done. The more I used it, the more it stopped feeling like a curse and more like a superpower. Something mine. Something I deserved.

Then gym class happened—and that's when I really went overboard.

It was basketball day, and Coach Renner decided to split us into teams for a full-court match. Normally, I was okay at basketball, not great. I could shoot sometimes, run fast, but I wasn't what you'd call team-carrying. But today, with PAUSE at my fingertips, I was about to become a legend.

The first time I paused during the game was when I got bored waiting for someone to pass me the ball. So, I froze time, moved into a better position, and un-paused it. Ball came flying to me. Perfect. Easy two-pointer. Nobody noticed.

The second time was when a guy from the other team was about to block one of our players. I paused, gently turned his shoulders so he faced the wrong way, and PLAY. He ran off in the opposite direction like a video game character glitching out. I had to bite my lip to keep from laughing. The game was becoming more like chess, and I was moving the pieces.

By the fifth pause, I was getting creative—rearranging our team into perfect formation whenever we had possession. I'd stop everything, move people just a few feet this way or that way, and then press PLAY so that it all looked natural. The passes got smoother. We were always open. We started winning hard, like, way harder than made sense. No one could figure out how we suddenly got so good.

By the eighth time, I didn't even hesitate. I paused when the ball was mid-air, adjusted people's arms so their catches would be cleaner, pushed defenders just slightly out of the way, even tied someone's shoelaces together because he kept elbowing me under the hoop. I felt invincible. Unstoppable.

Then it happened. The tenth time.

Jason, one of our better shooters, was going for a dramatic three-pointer. I watched the ball leave his hands and immediately saw the angle—it was off. Way off. Everyone held their breath, but I knew it wasn't going in. So I hit PAUSE, dashed across the court while everyone was frozen in a weird tense ballet, leapt up, grabbed the ball mid-air, and dunked it cleanly into the hoop. I even did a little victory pose before jogging back to my spot.

Grinning, I reached up and hit PLAY—but nothing happened.

I hit it again. Harder this time. Still nothing. The world stayed frozen. Jason was still mid-jump. Coach's whistle was inches from his lips. Even the scoreboard timer was stuck at 03:57. My stomach twisted. I hit the button over and over again, jabbing at it like it would wake up if I just tried hard enough. But it didn't. It was stuck. I was stuck.

Suddenly, the silence felt different. Heavier. Like I was trapped in a painting I couldn't leave. For the first time all day, I felt panic creep into my chest. I wasn't a time-controlling superhero anymore—I was a girl who might've broken the world by cheating at gym class.

And worst of all, no one could help me. Because no one else could move.

I tried everything I could think of. Pressing both PAUSE and PLAY at the same time. Holding them down. Swiping at the air around me in case there was some kind of invisible reset button. Nothing worked. The buttons floated above my head, unchanged. The world around me stayed stuck in perfect silence, like someone had taken a screenshot of reality and pasted me inside it.

I started yelling—not because I thought anyone would hear me, but because I didn't know what else to do. My voice bounced off the walls of the gym, echoing back at me with no one to answer. Jason hung in the air like a puppet on invisible strings, mouth open, hands still raised from his three-point attempt.

My teammates were mid-cheer. Coach Renner was just starting to blow her whistle. Everyone looked so alive… and yet so completely unreachable.

It was only then I realized how often I'd used the pause. How I'd tossed it around like it was a toy. Ten times in one day—ten major edits to the timeline, ten rewrites to reality. Maybe this power, this "curse," came with rules. Maybe I had broken one. Or maybe it was testing me. Punishing me.

I felt something deep in my chest, a pressure I hadn't noticed all day—like guilt that had been slowly building behind my ribs. I walked through the gym in slow motion, even though I was the only one moving. I studied their faces, every little detail.

A bead of sweat was frozen on my friend Lily's forehead. Her eyes wide, mouth open, about to cheer, I wondered if she would remember anything, if this would all unfreeze and she'd just see a miracle dunk. Or… would I be trapped here forever, left to wander through a world that no longer responded?

A terrible thought struck me: What if this was it? What if pressing PAUSE too many times didn't just stop time—it kicked me out of it? What if I had removed myself from the normal flow of the day, like a player glitching through a video game wall and falling into a void? Was I stuck between seconds?

I slumped against the wall and stared at the glowing buttons. The PAUSE button still shimmered faintly. The PLAY button looked duller now, like it was tired. Broken. I tried speaking to it. "Come on. Just one more time. I'll stop messing around. I won't use it unless I really need to." Nothing. Just silence and the hum of the gym lights. I hated how loud that silence felt when nothing else moved.

Then I did something kind of desperate. I started rewinding my steps, walking back across the gym to where I had jumped and dunked Jason's bad shot. The ball still rested in the net, stuck in place. I reached up and carefully pulled it out, then tried to float it back toward Jason's hands. It wasn't perfect, but I positioned it so it looked like it was still flying through the air, like it hadn't been interfered with. Like it never was a dunk.

I walked back to my original spot, the one I had moved from. I stood there and looked around. I whispered, "Undo." Then I waited. Still nothing. So I whispered, "I'm sorry." And for some reason, that felt heavier than anything I'd done all day. Because I meant it. I'd treated this like a game. I cheated. Not just at basketball—but at life. And I didn't realize until the moment I was locked out of it.

Suddenly, the PLAY button flickered.

It was faint at first, like a dying flashlight. But then it began to glow brighter. Slowly. Warmly. I held my breath and pressed it, this time with both hands, gently—not like a demand, but like a question. There was a click, a hum, and the sound of time came rushing back like a wave crashing into shore.

Jason's shot missed, bouncing off the rim. Gasps and groans filled the gym. The coach blew the whistle. The ball bounced once, twice, before someone picked it up. Everything was moving again. No one noticed I'd been gone. No one realized time had stopped. The world had forgiven me. Or maybe it had just decided I'd learned enough—for now.

I didn't touch the PAUSE button for the rest of the day. It hovered above me, patient and waiting, like a loaded question I wasn't ready to answer again. I walked home that afternoon with my backpack heavy and my heart heavier. I didn't know what curse would come tomorrow—but I knew now that some powers don't feel like curses until you misuse them.

And the scariest part? This was just Day One.

SIX

13 AND THRIVING

I'm never happy to hear the sound of my alarm clock ringing but today morning I was so excited to hear it. It was my 13th birthday; I was officially a teen. I had planned everything. There's an amusement park which is also partly a waterpark called 'Adventure Bay'. I was going to go there during the day with my best friends, Emma and Kaylee and then they would have a sleepover at my house. What more could anyone want on their 13th birthday?

I'm super excited to go to school today, despite the fact that it's a Monday. All kids have Monday Morning Blues sometimes but today I wasn't going through any of that. I love everything about celebrating my birthday in school except for when the birthday song plays during the assembly and I have to go to the front of the class.

It's not that I don't like getting wished by everyone. It's just that I would prefer if people actually came up to me and wished me personally, that way I would know if they actually care about me or just want chocolates.

Anyway, many people in my school like me. I'm pretty sure nobody despises me, other than the bullies. But who cares- the bullies despise everyone.

I go to school and hope that Mr. West forgets my birthday or just doesn't look at the birthday list. Our school has this unique thing called a birthday list. It's basically a month-wise list with every single student's name and birthday written on it.

Just like every normal school, you have to stand up in class while the assembly happens on the speakers. The assembly is going to have a thought of the day, a hymn, announcements, the school song, national anthem and worst of all- the birthday song.

Every day when it's time for the birthday song, Mr. West is going to go up to the birthday list on the wall and if it is someone's birthday he's going to say, "Oh happy birthday my dear. Come up to the front of the class. Let's sing for you." If its not anyone's birthday, he'll say, "Aww shucks, no birthdays. Its ok, let's sing because someone out in the world might have their special day today."

So I went to school. I was trembling throughout the entire assembly. Then came the time for the birthday song. Luckily Mr. West didn't check the list. Just as I was getting my hopes up, he says, "Anna! Happy birthday. Why didn't you tell us. Come on up to the front of the class." I tried denying it but it didn't work.

Mr. West is a little old fashioned but I love how he cares for each one of us. I mean, back in the day, kids would be so excited to go up to the front of the class. They would feel as if they ruled the world and everyone was praising them on their birthday. But now, us kids are just embarrassed by it because we know that we aren't gaining anything by going up front. We absolutely hate the fact of everyone staring at us.

All we know is that people keep a smile on their face so they can get extra chocolates. But I'm one person who is not going to let that slide. Not a single extra chocolate will be given under any conditions.

People say that on your birthday, time flies by as quick as possible. But it was the exact opposite. Each lesson is supposed to be 35 minutes but I couldn't even get past the first lesson, 10 minutes felt like an hour. I was completely zoned out when Mr. West called on me.

Math is one of my strong subjects though, so I wasn't worried. Whatever the question was, I believed I could answer it. But Becky thinks of herself as a queen and just really loudly and out of turn said, "Sir! She doesn't know the answer. She doesn't even know what the question is. Don't go easy on her because it's her birthday. But you can ask me. I know the answer." Before Mr. West could even say anything, I saw the question written on the board. It read, "What is the difference between a rational number and a fraction?"

I grab a marker, go up to the board an write the absolute correct answer. Just because I wrote the answer in my own words and also added an example, Becky disagreed. She said that it wasn't the same definition written in the book and the question doesn't ask for an example. I was so mad at her that I actually could throw a punch at her, but I didn't. Seeing my face turn red, Mr. West told Becky to cut it out.

Then we have singing as the next lesson. Its really relaxing so I was hoping to have some time to calm down, relax and sing to my favorite songs. The songs we generally sing to in music class are K-pop, hip-hop, rock, pop, country, new-age songs.... almost everything, just not opera. Opera is actually where I draw the line. Like I said earlier, this generation is not like the millennial times of previous generations. They loved this kind of music but we're into the new stylish and cool stuff.

Sometimes we also play guess the song during music class, that's what we did today. It's always boys versus girls. The girls always win but last time, the boys won and we were only one point apart. It was our goal to beat them this time. We get one point for guessing the song and we get 2 points if we also get the artist right. So, let the challenge begin.

The boys were off to a good start but the girls were too. By the end of the lesson, the girls had guessed, 'APT., love me like you do, blinding lights, kill this love, bang bang bang, summer of 69, beat it, what makes you beautiful, DJ got us falling in love' and many more songs. Let's just say the boys were not close at all, and we won.

The rest of the school day was pretty boring so, there's no point talking about it. Plus, I don't want to talk about it because for the rest of the day, I was in for a full-on party.

We got ready and went to Adventure Bay. We went on rollercoasters with so many loop-the-loops, there was one rollercoaster in which your seat would keep you upside-down and then you would go through loops and triple twists. There was this one ride which we didn't know was a waterslide or rollercoaster because there was water coming on us from all sides but the seats and track were that of a rollercoaster. We ran around the entire park and had so much fun. We got stuck in like 3 waterslides and it was so difficult to get out but that's exactly what made it so awesome.

We even sat in the wave pool and watched the movies-Captain America: Civil War and Avengers: Endgame because that's what they were playing on the big screen. All 3 of us were anyways fans of Marvel. Before these 2 movies they were playing Star Wars: The Force Awakens, but we couldn't make it on time because we were on all the rides.

We got potato wedges, french fries, chicken nuggets, pizza and pasta to eat. All of us also got our own drinks in a tumbler. I got coke, Emma got Fanta and Kaylee got Sprite. This is proof that if you're at the right place, at the right time, with the right people, you can have the best birthday ever even without a cake.

My mom called us to check up on us and see if we were doing ok, I told her, "Mom, we're not ok. We're absolutely slay and we're having the most fantastic time of our lives. I have to admit, Adventure Bay is awesome. I mean, it's bringing us the coolest adventure." My mom is very chill with me and my friends staying at a park alone because Emma is also 13 years old and Kaylee is 14. Kaylee didn't get held back, she's just older because she's been going to schools all around the world in different countries and they have different age groups in different schools.

After a bunch of fun, we finally decide to go back home because we were extremely tired. We go home to find the Entire house decorated with ballons and a banner saying, 'Happy Birthday Anna!" There are also 2 cakes just lying on the table. One was lit with candles and decorated fully; the other was just a plain icing cake. I wonder what the 2 cakes are for. Little did I know, Emma and Kaylee already knew that my parents had set this up and that they were hiding behind the curtains.

So, just as I walk towards the cakes, my parents come out from their hiding spot. Emma, Kaylee, my mom and my dad just push my entire face into the plain icing cake and scream, "Happy 13th birthday Anna! You're officially a teenager!" The second I get my face out of the cake; they hand me a knife to cut the other decorated cake with candles and start singing the birthday song right after I blow out the candles. Now, this is the birthday song that I like, the lyrics are the same but this one isn't embarrassing and just has the real birthday vibe.

We click a bunch of pictures and then I go wash my face. All of us change into our nightdresses and eat cake while watching Harry Potter and The Deathly Hallows. After my parents go to sleep, we do each other's makeup, eat some more cake and binge watch (technically re-watch) all the episodes of Wednesday Addams.

At least now I know why there were 2 cakes. 1 to push my face into and 1 to actually eat. These parties with my parents and 2 BFFs never get old. On Saturday, I also have another party planned but this time with all of my friends. Generally, I would be excited for that, but I'm too tired to get ready for another day of complete fun. Because we're going to stay awake all night (I hope). Saturday is only 3 days away, I can wait, I'm pretty sure I also need a break for a couple of days. I just hope I don't get my face smudged into cake again any time soon. Anyways, that's a thought for another day. Right now, I just had the best day of my life.

It was the ultimate birthday bash; we splashed, screamed and slept over. It was the birthday that had it all: - rides, slides and sleepovers. I guess you could say that I'm 13 AND THRIVING.

SEVEN

From The Shadows to The Spotlight

I was bored at school and since it was a free period, we had nothing to do. "Ok class, today we have a new student joining us", said Mrs. Smith. A tall, handsome boy with sleek brown hair walked up to the front of the class. "He seems really weird.", murmured one of the kids. The boy and Mrs. Smith heard the kid say that which I could notice made the boy feel uncomfortable in his new class. Mrs. Smith comforted him by saying, "Don't worry about the other kids. Some of them can be pretty rude but its ok, you'll make friends. Now come on, introduce yourself. Go ahead."

The boy stumbled at first looking at all the students staring at him but he gained the confidence to speak up. He said, "Hi guys, my name is Choi Min-Jun. I'm from South Korea." There was an uprising of questions from the class. The boy that teased him earlier said, "Hey, I'm Steve Anderson. So why did you shift here?" Everybody including me, gave Steve looks while his friends smirked thinking about what Min-jun's reply would be. Steve has always been a bully, I assumed he was going to annoy Min-jun just as much as he annoys the rest of us by his so called 'funny insults'. Min-jun explained that he had to move to the U.S. because his father got a job promotion.

If I was shifting to another country, even I would feel judged by others. So just when I noticed the pressure on Min-jun, I decided to ask him a question to decrease the tension in the air, "What does your name mean. I think it sounds damn cool." He smiled at me and said, "Min-jun is divided into 2 syllables. Min as in clever and Jun meaning talented, so...clever and talented. My last name Choi meaning mountain peak reflects strength and stability." I signaled him that he could sit next to me.

He looked scared, who wouldn't be? I can't believe that Steve has the audacity to make him feel worse when he's just an innocent kid like the rest of us. Well, some of us aren't exactly innocent, you could call them a bit dirty minded but that doesn't matter. I made it my responsibility to make Min-jun fit in the school. Isn't that what first friends are for?

During recess, both of us sat on a bench under an old mango tree, right in front of the football field. We were eating our lunches and talking, you know, just the normal stuff. The thing is he seemed like a really nice guy and I wanted to get to know him really well.

But seconds later, my 14-year-old curiosity kicked in. I just had to ask Min-jun, "So, do all Korean names have the last name before the first name? No offense or anything, I just wanted to know." I felt so embarrassed after that and told him that it was fine if he felt uncomfortable answering the question. Min-jun laughed, reassured me that he was fine with me asking that and told me that mostly it is like that. I mean, you don't really get to meet a lot of Koreans, and I love K-pop and K-dramas so it felt pretty awesome.

We got to know each other a lot, and even got paired together for a group project for which they were going to meet at the park after school. Min-jun's day was pretty decent for a new kid.

He reached the park early but didn't notice that I was sitting at the complete opposite side. He saw that Steve was also there and he immediately ran to hide. Steve screamed out, "Guys, guess what?! The Korean kid from school is here." As he walked towards Min-jun, he said that he wanted a fresh start. Min-jun didn't trust him but played along. I saw all of this but didn't interfere. I wanted to see if Min-jun could stand up for himself, of course he could but I just didn't want to make it worse.

Steve asked, "Hmm, you know something about you felt a little off. What do you wanna be when you grow up?" Min-jun just got up and told Steve that he was busy and was waiting for someone. Steve forced him to answer the question. Min-jun said he wanted to be a rapper. Steve and his gang laughed. Min-jun said, "oh really, you wanna hear one?"

Cause you're a bully, you make everyone scatter,
No need to be proud, no need to be flattered.
My life's a mess, my nerves are bad,
The names you call me, they hurt real bad.
I need some love, I need some time,
I disguise myself and act like I'm fine.
Its all cause of you, cause you don't care,
How about don't be a bully and make things fair.
In your head, you think you're really cool,
But in reality, you're just a damn fool.

Steve kicks Min-jun in the stomach but he throws back a punch and says with confidence, "You think I can't put up a fight, huh? Don't underestimate me just cause I'm Korean." Till then I've had enough. I go up to Steve and say, "He's not wrong you know? You're a bully and don't care about anyone. Someday you might regret bullying him. So cut it out!" Steve mimics me and leaves, but I honestly don't care.

I tell Min-jun that he can come over to my house for the project and I could also give him an ice pack. I can tell that the way Steve kicked him must've hurt real bad. We walk slowly to my house and have a small chat on the way too.

"Mackenzie, why'd you stand up for me?"

"Why not? I believe that you can be an awesome rapper one day."

"Wow, nobody's ever given me hope like that. People just try to destroy the hope that I barely have left."

"That's exactly what Steve was doing. Deep-down even you know that you can do this."

"Thanks."

We reach my house and we open up the chemistry activity book. There are a million experiments that we can do for the project. Min-jun gets a little freaked out about it. I tell him that we can have something to eat and go over the topics. Eventually we choose a classic- the baking soda volcano. We burn the midnight oil but it pays off because we get an A+.

The next day, the first lesson we have is P.E. Mr. Johnson calls out attendance, "raise your hand and say present if you're here. After that I'll be putting you all in teams for throwball." We do the daily drill and get started on making teams. Mr. Johnson says the teams out loud, "Choi Min-jun, Ava Walker, Troy Allen, William Parker and Mackenzie Rodriguez on Team A. Robbie Patterson, Brooke Torres, Jake

Evans, Steve Anderson, Sydney Rogers and Bailey Bryant on Team B. The rest of you guys go for basketball, I'll meet you guys after I'm done setting up throwball. OK CLASS! Teams, take your sides and begin!"

Min-jun innocently asks while trying to hold his smirks, "Woah your last name is Rodriguez?!" I reply with laughter and teasingly say, "Shut up. And yeah, it is."

Team A decided their positions on the basis of how good someone is so Troy, Ava, and I go up front but during the game when Team A starts losing, everyone loses hope. But Min-jun catches all the balls Team B throws at them and returns them with perfect throws. Eventually Team A wins not knowing Min-jun's capacity and ability. Steve throws a tantrum saying that it can't be possible but everyone tells him that it is what it is.

Years pass by the same way. Me and Min-jun become better friends. Min-jun also keeps on practicing his rapping skills along with his studies and sports. He turns out to be good at almost everything. He comes over to my place or we go to his place and have fun.

We also become study buddies. I even help him by motivating him that he can achieve his dreams. Sometimes just for fun, I would also try saying his raps but I would end up saying gibberish because I have singing skills but I'm not that good at rapping. We give each other feedback on each other's songs and lyrics.

As we graduate, Min-jun gets the highest score anyone in the school has ever gotten. I was so happy that day because I also came second. After that we continued our work towards our careers but we still remained best friends. We did many collab songs and recordings too.

Min-jun does grow up to be a rapper, one of the best in the entire world of K-pop. He also starrs in multiple movies and k-dramas. At his debut concert, just as we're going backstage, we bump into a person who can't find his way. I'm able to recognize him. It was Steve from high school. Turns out Steve became a fan of his music and was his biggest fan- he knew all his songs. Steve apologized for everything that happened amongst them in the past and Min-jun being a good person accepted his apology.

Although Min-jun made his mark as the most successful Korean star in all of history, he still spends time with me, not letting the fame get to his head and also gives me credit for helping and motivating him throughout his career. I also went on stage that day for one of our collab songs. We work towards doing even better in the future. We had to go to different places for our concerts all around the world. We talked less but remained in contact and still didn't drift apart.

In one of Min-jun's interviews, he says, "Find true friends and stay by their side forever. That's one thing I've learnt because my best friend Mackenzie stood by me since high school. You don't need a million fake friends; you just need one loyal friend. Make sure that in search of gold, you don't lose a diamond." It was the happiest day of my life when I saw that interview. So all you need is the support of one person to accomplish your dreams.

EIGHT

HUMAN OR GHOST: TRUE LOVE LIVES FOREVER

It was one of those rare afternoons where the weather was perfect—not too hot, not too cool—just right for a quiet walk in the garden. I'd been feeling a bit overwhelmed lately, so I thought some time among the flowers might help clear my head.

The scent of blooming jasmine and the soft hum of bees buzzing around made the whole place feel like a dream. I wandered deeper into the garden path, taking my time with each step, until I nearly bumped into someone standing near a patch of bright orange marigolds.

"Oh, sorry!" I said, stepping back quickly. He turned to face me with an easy smile and didn't look annoyed at all. In fact, he looked more curious than anything. "Hey, I've seen you before," he said, narrowing his eyes slightly. "Do you go to Pacific High?" I hesitated for a second, surprised, and then nodded. "Yeah, I do," I replied. He smiled like he'd solved a small mystery. "I thought so. I'm Ashton," he added, offering a hand casually.

We stood there for a moment, a little awkward but not uncomfortable. Something about him felt familiar, though I couldn't quite place where I'd seen him. He gestured toward the open grassy area a few feet away. "Want to sit?" I nodded, and we made our way to a spot where the sun streamed down in golden rays. The grass was warm beneath us, and the flowers swayed gently in the breeze like they were eavesdropping on us.

"So," I began, glancing over at him, "how come I've never noticed you at school?" He chuckled. "I kind of keep to myself. Plus, I'm not in any sports or clubs or anything. But I've seen you around—library, I think."

That made me smile. I'd spent more time than I'd like to admit hiding out in the library during lunch. It felt nice, knowing someone had noticed, even if I hadn't noticed them back.

The conversation flowed easier after that. We talked about classes, teachers, the weird kid who always brings a bird to school.

Ashton had this quiet, thoughtful way of speaking that made me feel like he really listened. I found myself relaxing more than I had in days. By the time the sun started dipping behind the trees, it felt like I'd known him for a lot longer than just one afternoon.

The sun hung low in the sky, casting golden light across the garden as we sat beneath the old oak tree. Laughter floated between us, light and easy, as Ashton recounted a story from class that had both of us in stitches.

The warm breeze and gentle rustling of leaves made time feel like it had slowed to a crawl. But when I casually glanced down at my wrist and saw the time glowing on my watch face, a jolt of panic ran through me. It was much later than I had thought — I was supposed to be home nearly an hour ago.

As I stood up abruptly and began brushing grass from my jeans, Ashton looked at me, confused. "You heading out?" he asked, rising to his feet. I nodded quickly, slinging my bag over my shoulder. "Yeah, I didn't realize how late it had gotten," I said, already taking a step toward the garden gate.

He took a half-step forward, hesitant. "Hey — I didn't catch your name," he added with a small smile. I paused, then turned back, matching his smile. "It's Abigail," I said, "but everyone just calls me Abby." His smile widened, and I could tell he filed it away in his mind.

The next afternoon, the bell rang at school and my thoughts immediately went to the garden. I didn't have to wonder if Ashton would be there — something told me he would be.

Sure enough, as I walked through the bushes and flowers towards the corner of the garden, there he was, sitting cross-legged with a small chess set spread out between us. "I figured you'd be back," he said with a grin. I laughed and dropped my bag beside him, settling into the grass. "You figured right."

As we played, Ashton leaned back on his hands and looked over at me. "So, I did a little research last night," he said, moving a knight across the board. "Turns out, Abigail was a name often used for Hawaiian princesses."

I raised my eyebrows, both amused and curious. "Really?" I said, looking up from the board. He nodded.

"Yeah — and I think it suits you. You're kind of like a princess." The words were casual, but his gaze was steady. I felt my cheeks flush with warmth, and I looked down at the chessboard to hide the smile tugging at my lips.

We played a few more rounds, the game slipping in and out of focus as our conversation drifted from books to music to the weird things our teachers said in class.

The garden around us buzzed gently with the sounds of late spring — bees among the flowers, birds chirping in the trees. Despite the hours passing, this time I didn't check my watch.

I didn't want to know how late it was. For now, I was content to just be Abby, sitting across from Ashton in a quiet garden where everything felt a little more magical than usual.

Eventually, we closed the chess set and just sat there staring at the beautiful sunset. I couldn't get my eyes off of it until Ashton suddenly said, "You know, it's just like you."

I gave him a confused look. He sighed, "You're just as pretty as the sunset. And..." He stumbled, "I can't take my eyes off the sunset just like I can't take my eyes off you." I wasn't mad at him for saying any of it, I just replied, "Stop being so flirty.", I gave him a slight push.

He completely fell backwards and pretended as if that push actually hurt him. I rolled my eyes; I don't really like dramatic boys. I ignored his stupid actions and continued looking at the sunset. Just the second I turned my eyes away from him, he fell on me and both of us went rolling down the small slope of the garden.

When we came to a stop, neither of us could hold it in and burst out in laughter. It was a pretty fun experience; I don't think I would have enjoyed it that much if it was with somebody else.

We stared into each other's eyes while smiling for at least a minute. It was at that moment that I realised I had fallen in love with Ashton. I turned away slightly; he asked me what was wrong but I just brushed it off by saying that I was tired.

On the other hand, the voice inside my head was screaming at me, "SERIOUSLY?! YOU FELL IN LOVE WITH A BOY YOU JUST MET YESTERDAY!" I actually didn't blame the voice in my head but I just knew that Ashton was different from everybody else. I like being around people who are just as social as me. Although Ashton was completely introverted, something about him just felt right.

I decided to think about when I got home. I was doing my homework, but all I could think about was Ashton. When I was watching a movie or listening to songs, the only thing I could think about was still Ashton. Love at first sight is difficult to deal with and I'm not joking when I say that; I just couldn't get him out of my head.

The next day after school, I made my way to the garden like always, drawn by the comfort it had come to hold — and because Ashton was there. I found him sitting by the fence, quietly watching the breeze ruffle the petals of the flowers we had seen bloom together for months.

Something had been nagging at me, so I asked him why none of the teachers ever called his name during class. He gave me a soft, tired look and said he thought it was a prank. According to him, some seniors had been pulling this elaborate joke on him for over a year — even the teachers were in on it. I didn't know what to make of that, but before I could ask more, he led me to the corner of the garden we'd always called "ours."

When we got there, I stopped short. A mat was laid out with our favourite snacks, some candles, and in the centre

— a bouquet of fresh flowers. Ashton picked it up and turned to me with a nervous smile. "Abigail Stevenson," he said, "will you be my girlfriend?"

My heart leapt. I'd loved him for so long and hearing him ask made everything fall into place. I said yes. I remember how his eyes lit up, how the world seemed a little more golden in that moment.

But that night, something unsettled me. The prank story didn't sit right. The way people ignored him, how he never showed up on class rosters — it all felt... off.

So, I started researching. I typed his name, Ashton Allen, into every search engine I could find. For days, nothing came up but one strange, repeating article: a local news report about a teenage boy who had been murdered on school grounds the previous year. No photos, no further details. Just a haunting story that sent chills down my spine.

I was beginning to hope it was just coincidence — that maybe there was another Ashton Allen — until I found an old blog post from a student archive. It had a picture attached. And there he was; Ashton; My Ashton. The boy in the photo had the same soft eyes, the same smile, standing in front of the garden where we always met. My heart stopped.

For the next week, I could barely look at him without my chest tightening. He didn't know. He couldn't know. He would tell me about plans for the weekend, about songs he liked, about the future he wanted with me — and I'd smile and nod like nothing was wrong. But inside, I was breaking.

Every time he reached for my hand, it felt colder. Every time I heard him laugh; it sounded more distant. Finally, I couldn't take it anymore. I asked him to meet me in our garden one last time.

When he arrived, he looked worried, like he could feel something was coming. I took his hand and gently told him everything. That he'd been gone for over a year. That no one else could see or hear him. That he was... a ghost.

At first, he laughed like I was joking. But as I showed him the articles, the photo, the date of his death, the light in his eyes flickered. He went quiet for a long time, just staring at the flowers in his hand. "I didn't know," he whispered.

And then, as if the truth had freed him, his figure started to fade, like fog in the morning sun. I reached out, but he was already gone. I stood there, alone in our garden, holding the bouquet he gave me — the petals still warm.

All I know and believe is that he's probably in a better place now. I hoped for a future with him, just like he hoped for one with me. Now I'll never know if I'll find love like that ever again.

When I'm feeling down nowadays, the only thing that brings me up is the thought of him; the thought that one day I might join him and we'll get our happy ending. Till this day, not a single second goes by when I don't think of him and I'm pretty sure he knows that.

NINE

SISTER OR STRANGER?

It all started on a Thursday evening. I remember it clearly—not because anything special had happened earlier that day, but because of what I saw that night. My phone was running dangerously low on battery, and like always, I suspected my sister, Lizzie, had taken my charger. She always "borrowed" it and conveniently forgot to return it. So I got up, dragging my feet across the carpeted hallway, grumbling to myself about how annoying little sisters could be.

When I reached her room, I didn't bother knocking. We had an unspoken rule of barging in on each other whenever we wanted, and I was too tired to be polite. But as I pushed open the door just a crack, something stopped me dead in my tracks.

There, in the dim glow of her fairy lights, was Lizzie... or at least something that used to look like her. Her skin was no longer the soft, peachy color I'd grown up seeing. It was green—vibrant in places and dull in others, sort of like old copper. Her hair, usually tangled and curly, floated upward slightly as if she were underwater. And she was muttering to herself in a language that didn't sound human. It wasn't French or Spanish or even some obscure dialect—this was... otherworldly. Clicking sounds, guttural growls, and sharp syllables I'd never heard before filled the room.

I didn't move. I didn't breathe. My hand was still on the doorknob, my heart pounding so loud I was sure she could hear it. But she didn't. She didn't even turn around. Whatever she was doing had her full attention. Slowly, silently, I backed away and closed the door.

At first, I thought maybe I was dreaming. I genuinely questioned if I had fallen asleep with my phone in my hand and imagined the whole thing. But then it happened again. The next evening, right around the same time, I walked past her room, curiosity getting the better of me, and peeked in.

Same green skin. Same strange language. Still facing away from me. And for three days after that, it happened again and again. I became obsessed with it—watching her from that narrow slit in the doorway. I didn't dare go inside. I didn't speak to her about it. During the day, she acted normal. She was Lizzie—the same annoying, goofy, sometimes sweet sister I'd always known. But at night, she was something else.

One night, I saw something that made me question everything I thought I understood about the universe. I caught her in the middle of transforming. She was lying on her bed, scrolling through TikTok, looking completely normal. I blinked. And then... she changed. Not slowly. Not subtly. One moment, she was human, and the next, she was that thing. Green skin, strange eyes, floating hair. It was like watching a glitch in reality. My heart practically slammed against my ribcage.

Still, I didn't tell her I knew. I couldn't. I was scared out of my mind. But the worst part—the moment that truly shook me—was the night I finally saw her face from the front.

She turned around. Just slightly. Just enough for me to see her profile. And that was all it took. Her face was wrinkled and old-looking, like a dried leaf, even though she was only thirteen. The green wasn't consistent anymore; there were blotches of blue near her jaw and temples. And her eyes—God, her eyes. They were completely black. Not just the pupils. No white. No color. Just two ink-black orbs staring straight ahead. Cold. Empty. Alien.

I stumbled back from the door and nearly screamed. I had to bite my hand to keep myself quiet. That night, I couldn't sleep. I lay awake with my blanket pulled up to my chin, eyes wide open, wondering what I had just witnessed.

Of course, I told my parents.

Well, tried to. That weekend, I sat them down after dinner and said, "I think there's something seriously wrong with Lizzie." They gave each other that look—the look parents give when they're trying not to laugh at something they don't understand.

"Carrie," Mom said patiently, "you've got such an imagination. Is this some kind of spooky Halloween prank you're setting up early?"

I shook my head violently. "No! I'm serious! I've seen her—she changes at night. She's not... she's not human."

"Sweetie," Dad chimed in, "You've been watching too many of those weird alien documentaries again. Lizzie is fine. She's just a kid."

But I knew what I saw. And it didn't feel like a prank. At first, I even considered the possibility that it was one—Lizzie was the queen of pranks, after all. Last year she made everyone think our microwave was haunted by hiding a Bluetooth speaker inside it and playing ghostly whispers. But this? This was too much. Too real. The transformation wasn't fake. Her eyes alone—how would you even fake that?

I argued with my mom about it every single day. After school, before dinner, after dinner. She got tired of it and eventually started brushing me off with a quick, "We'll talk about this later." But "later" never came. I tried telling my friends. They laughed at first, then grew uncomfortable, and finally started ignoring me. I overheard them whispering behind my back in the hallways—"She thinks her sister's an alien," followed by giggles and eyerolls.

So I stopped talking. And I started recording.

Every night, like clockwork, I would sneak over to Lizzie's door and start filming. I made sure the sound was on. I caught the weird language, the strange humming noise she made, the faint glow that seemed to come from her body. I got videos of her skin changing color. One night, I even caught her mid-transformation again—perfectly, with a timestamp and everything. It took about a month, but by then, I had enough footage to fill a whole folder labeled "LIZZIE—ALIEN PROOF."

The night I showed my parents the videos was one I'll never forget.

At first, they watched in silence. Then, slowly, their faces changed. My mom's jaw dropped. My dad blinked like he couldn't believe what he was seeing. And then, finally, my mom whispered, "What... the hell..."

That's when Lizzie walked in.

She looked at the screen, looked at us, and then said, "I guess it's time I told you the truth."

The explanation was bizarre—but somehow, it all made sense. Lizzie wasn't really from Earth. She was from a colony on Jupiter, sent to Earth on a certified mission to study human life. Apparently, adoption made for the perfect cover. She'd been blending in, collecting data, and transmitting it back home during those nightly transformations. She said she never meant to scare anyone, and she truly did love us like a real family.

My parents were stunned. I don't think they fully believed it until she transformed right there in front of them, slowly, without fear. My mom gasped. My dad swore. But they didn't yell. They didn't run. They just... stared.

In the end, they told her she couldn't stay. Not because they didn't love her. But because it felt wrong to keep secrets that big, especially ones that could endanger us—or her. They said she needed to return to Jupiter and finish her mission properly. They couldn't have an alien "snooping around" their house, as my dad put it.

Lizzie didn't protest. She had always talked about moving out someday, anyway. I guess this was just like that—except this time, she wasn't moving to another city. She was leaving the planet.

When she left, I cried. We all did. Even my dad. It felt like a hole had been ripped out of our family. Sure, she was adopted. Sure, she was from another world. But she was still my sister. The one who stole my charger, who played stupid pranks, who sang way too loud in the shower.

Now, the room down the hall is empty. Sometimes, I sit on her bed and look up at the stars. I wonder if she's watching us from up there. I wonder if she misses us.

Some truths change everything. And some truths... you just have to live with.

TEN

FAMILY CIRCUIT

It had been raining since morning. Not the light, gentle kind of rain that makes you feel calm — this was the heavy, grey kind that made everything outside look like a black-and-white movie.

I sat by the window, my chin resting on my hand, watching raindrops race each other down the glass. The sky was a thick blanket of clouds, and the steady thump of raindrops hitting the roof made the house feel even quieter than usual. It was one of those days where time felt like it was moving in slow motion.

I sighed and reached over to grab my iPad. Maybe watching a few videos or playing a game would help pass the time. But of course — just my luck — the screen stayed black.

I held the power button longer, but nothing. Dead; I tossed it onto my bed with a groan and sat back, staring at the ceiling like it had answers. The rain kept falling. It wasn't just a boring day — it was a 'stuck-inside-with-nothing-to-do' kind of day.

After a moment, I reached under my bed and pulled out my old sketchbook and a freshly sharpened pencil. I hadn't drawn in a while, but something about the rain made me want to do it. It was quiet, and my room was filled with that cozy grey light that made everything feel soft.

I flipped through the pages until I found a blank one and stared at it for a moment. Then, an idea popped into my head — What if I had a robot friend? Not a clunky metal one, but a really cool one. Sleek, smart, and helpful. Just for fun, I started sketching.

At first, I just drew the outline — tall, with long arms and rounded shoulders. Then I added details: little joints where the fingers would move, a smooth visor for its eyes, and a small backpack-like panel that could open to store tools or snacks.

The pencil felt just right in my hand, gliding over the page like it knew what to do. I shaded the arms to give them a metallic shine and used short, smooth strokes to make the legs look strong but flexible. Every piece of the robot had a purpose. It wasn't just a random doodle — it was starting to feel real.

Hours passed without me noticing. The sound of the rain had become part of the background, like soft music. I kept drawing, fixing tiny details, shading the panels, and even giving the robot a small logo on its chest — a lightning bolt inside a circle.

When I finally sat back and looked at it, I smiled. It looked awesome. My robot stood tall on the page, one hand on its hip, the other raised in a wave. It had a friendly but cool look, like it could help me with homework and battle evil aliens if it needed to.

It was late — I could hear the clatter of dishes downstairs, and my stomach growled. I placed my sketchbook on the desk carefully and headed down for dinner.

As I sat at the table, Mom looked up from her plate and said, "What were you doing in your room for so long?" I grinned and said, "I was drawing a robot. Like, a friend robot. I spent the whole afternoon working on it." My voice was full of excitement, but before she could reply, my younger brother shouted, "BORING! Video games are so much better than drawing and stuff."

I rolled my eyes, but Mom just smiled and said calmly, "Well, I think it's wonderful you have a creative hobby. Your brother is just addicted to screens." She winked at me as she handed me a bowl of rice. I felt a little better.

Even though my brother thought drawing was lame, at least Mom got it. I stayed quiet for the rest of dinner, thinking about how real my robot had started to feel. It was just a drawing... but still, something about it felt different.

After dinner, I climbed the stairs back to my room, passing the window on the landing. Rain was still coming down, softer now, almost like a whisper. I stepped into my room and walked over to the window.

Through the wet glass, I could see into Marcus's house across the street. He was my neighbour and one of my best friends. He was lying on his bed, scrolling on his phone, looking just as bored as I had been earlier.

I picked up my phone and called him. A second later, he looked up and saw me waving. He smiled, then picked up. "Hi Mica", he said. "Hey", I replied. We talked for a while about our day. He told me he'd been trying to finish reading the second Percy Jackson book.

I told him all about the robot I had drawn and how I imagined having a robot friend who looked just like it. There was a pause, and then he said, "Imagine if it came to life. That would be awesome, right?" I laughed. "Yeah. That would be seriously awesome."

Eventually, we both said goodnight and hung up. I closed the curtains, stretched, and got into bed. My sketchbook was still on my desk, the robot staring up at the ceiling with its pencilled eyes.

As the rain tapped gently on the window and the wind whispered through the trees, I couldn't help but imagine... What if it really could come to life?

I wake up early in the morning and see something sitting on my chair. I sit up straight and rub my eyes to see it more clearly. It's the robot I had drawn. It sees me and comes up to me.

I heard my mom's footsteps coming up the stairs, and I barely had time to shove the robot into my closet. It whirred quietly, almost like it was trying to be polite, but I shot it a look anyway — be quiet.

I threw a blanket over the closet door just in case and tried to look like I'd just woken up. My mom poked her head into my room, smiled, and said, "Great, you're already up. Come down for breakfast in some time." I nodded and forced a smile. "Okay," I said, pretending everything was perfectly normal. She didn't notice anything weird, thank goodness, and headed back down the stairs.

At the table, I ate faster than I ever have in my life. I think I surprised everyone — even my dad raised an eyebrow. "Slow down, Mica," he said. "You're going to choke." But I just smiled and muttered something about being really hungry. The truth was, I couldn't stop thinking about the robot upstairs in my closet. The one I drew. The one that somehow came to life overnight.

I couldn't tell them, not my mom, not my dad, and definitely not my brother. They'd think I was either lying or losing it. Luckily, my parents didn't press me. After breakfast, they grabbed their coffee, said their goodbyes, and left for work like it was any normal day.

I knew my brother wouldn't be a problem — he was probably holed up in his room with his headphones on, shouting at some game. So, I rushed back upstairs and closed the door behind me. I picked up my phone and called Marcus. "You're not going to believe me," I told him, "But the robot I drew yesterday? It came to life." He didn't believe me, of course. Thought I was messing with him.

But after five straight minutes of me insisting I wasn't, he finally agreed to come over. When he arrived, I heard a thud outside my window and then saw him swing his legs through the frame. "You know we have a door, right?", I said. "Yeah," he grinned. "But climbing in through the window is kind of my thing."

Marcus stared at the robot in stunned silence for a solid minute before whispering, "Okay... you weren't lying." We both circled around it, like it might jump at us or vanish if we looked away. It was still, but its eyes blinked now and then, glowing faint blue.

"What do we do with it?" Marcus asked. That was the big question. I had no idea how it came to life, or what it wanted, or if it even wanted anything. But I knew one thing — if anyone else found out, it'd be taken away. Or worse. So, for now, it was just me, Marcus, and a robot that shouldn't exist, standing in the middle of my bedroom like it belonged there.

Before we could come up with any kind of plan, the robot shifted slightly and turned its head toward us. Marcus jumped back, nearly tripping over my chair, but I stood frozen, eyes wide.

Then it spoke — its voice smooth and clear, with a strange, almost musical tone. "Where am I?" it asked. Marcus looked at me, his mouth hanging open. I swallowed hard and stepped forward. "You're in my room," I said slowly. "My name's Mica. This is Marcus." The robot tilted its head, blinking a few times. "You created me," it said. Not asked — said. Like it already knew.

"How do you know that?" Marcus asked, finally finding his voice. The robot raised one hand and pointed to the sketchbook on my desk. "This was my origin. You imagined me, and the energy of that imagination brought me into being."

We both stared at each other, stunned. I hadn't even told it about the sketchbook. Marcus picked it up and flipped through the pages. "So... wait. If we draw something else, it'll come to life too?" The robot paused for a second. "Not everything. Only what is drawn with intent. With belief." That sent a chill down my spine. I hadn't meant for this to happen — not really. I was just doodling during a boring rainy day. Was that enough to count as belief?

I started firing off questions, barely taking a breath. "Do you have a name? Do you need anything to survive? Are there more like you?" The robot answered patiently, one by one. "I do not have a name unless you give me one. I do not require food or water, but I must be kept away from high electromagnetic interference. I am the only one currently. As for purpose — I was made to assist, protect, and explore."

Marcus whispered, "Okay, that last part sounds like some Iron Man-level stuff." I could barely hear him. My mind was spinning. I hadn't just made something cool — I might've made something important.

After a few minutes, we sat down across from it, trying to absorb everything. Marcus was already pulling out his phone to start writing ideas down. "We have to keep this secret," I said, serious now. "If anyone finds out—" "They won't," he interrupted, locking his phone and slipping it into his pocket. "This thing's ours now. We'll figure it out together."

I looked at the robot, at its sleek metal limbs and softly glowing eyes, and I felt something strange — responsibility. Like I'd just adopted a piece of the future, and now I had to protect it. "Alright," I said. "First things first... we need to give you a name."

Marcus suggested we just call him Robo because he's a robot. But I disagreed, it was a name we had been calling all robots ever since we were kids. Its too old fashioned. Robo wasn't that bad so I said that maybe we could name it Robbie, it's pretty close to Robo. Marcus agreed and so did Robbie.

Just as Marcus and I were deep in conversation, the door to my room creaked open. My little brother Danny stood there, rubbing his eyes like he'd just woken up, until he looked up and froze. "Goodness gracious! Who is that?" he shouted, pointing at Robbie. I jumped up and tried to block his view, but it was way too late for that. "This is Robbie," I said quickly, trying to think of some kind of cover. "Danny, this is Marcus. And that's—uh—my... science project." Danny raised one eyebrow in a way only he could. "You named it Robbie? Awesome. But I'm telling Mom and Dad."

I wanted to scream. My heart dropped to my stomach. The second my parents were back, Danny was already halfway down the stairs, yelling something about a robot in my room. I looked at Marcus, who just muttered, "We're doomed."

But a weird thing happened — Danny didn't just blurt out something crazy and random. He told them everything. Every single detail. The sketch, how it came to life, how we tried to keep it a secret. And the most shocking part? He got it right. Like, word for word. I was mad, sure, but also weirdly impressed.

My parents sat there, listening quietly. And when he was done... they didn't freak out. No yelling, no grounding, no phone calls to the government. Just a few silent stares between them and then my mom said, "Well, I guess we'll need to find a place for Robbie to stay."

Now, it's been two years since that day, and Robbie is just... part of the family. He sits with us during dinner (though he doesn't eat), helps Danny with homework, and even beat my dad at chess — twice.

Sometimes I look at him and still can't believe he's real, that he came from something I sketched in the corner of a sketchbook. Me and Marcus used to lose sleep worrying about what would happen if anyone found out. But the truth was, we didn't need to. Our family didn't run or panic. They just accepted it. Like Robbie belonged here all along.

Sometimes I wonder what would've happened if we'd kept hiding him. If we'd tried to cover everything up forever. But then I look at Danny, who treats Robbie like a big brother, or my mom, who reminds Robbie to "charge up" before bed, like it's just another chore. And I realize, maybe the world isn't always as scary as we think.

ELEVEN

A TIMELINE OF SECRETS

I still remember the chill of that winter evening when I received the call. Detective Jameson's voice was grim. "Emily, I need your help. We've got a body at the Richardson estate, and it's a mess."

I was a kid, a 16-year-old. Now, you'd be thinking why a Detective is calling me. Turns out, being smart not only helps in school but also helps in getting a part-time job.

I had a keen interest for mysteries, yet I couldn't be a detective. With the help of my senior officials, I became a forensic psychologist- this way I could still be a part of many cases at a young age.

I'd worked with the police department on several cases, but nothing could have prepared me for this. The Richardson family was prominent in our small town, and their patriarch, Henry Richardson, was a respected businessman.

Upon arrival, I saw the body – Henry Richardson, lying in his study, a single bullet wound to the chest. The room was in disarray, papers scattered everywhere. Jameson briefed me on the situation: the family had hosted a dinner party the night before, and the murder occurred sometime after the guests departed.

As I began my evaluation, I noticed something peculiar. The victim's wife, Catherine, seemed overly composed, almost detached. Their son, Alex, was visibly shaken, but his sister, Sophia, appeared almost...smug.

The investigation revealed a web of secrets and lies within the family. Henry had been blackmailing several business rivals, and his family stood to gain a substantial inheritance. Each family member had a motive, but one detail bothered me: the lack of forced entry or exit. It seemed the killer was someone the victim knew well.

As I dug deeper, I discovered a hidden safe in Henry's desk. Inside, there were cryptic notes and a recording. The voice on the tape sent chills down my spine: "You'll pay for what you've done."

The list of suspects narrowed down, but the evidence pointed to multiple individuals. I had to decipher the cryptic messages and unravel the complex family dynamics to uncover the truth.

With each new revelation, the picture became clearer, but the killer's identity remained elusive. One thing was certain – nothing was as it seemed, and the truth would be shocking.

As I continued my investigation, I became increasingly convinced that the key to solving the case lay in understanding the complex relationships within the Richardson family. I decided to conduct individual interviews with each family member, digging deeper into their motives and alibis.

Catherine, the wife, seemed hesitant to discuss her husband's business dealings, but I sensed a deep-seated tension beneath her composed exterior. "He was a hard man to live with," she said, her voice barely above a whisper. "But I loved him in my own way."

Alex, the son, revealed his father's ruthless tactics in the corporate world, his anger and resentment palpable. "He would stop at nothing to get what he wanted," Alex said, his eyes flashing with emotion. "I hated him for it."

Sophia, the daughter, appeared reluctant to share information, but her eyes betrayed a deep-seated anger. "He ruined my life," Sophia said, her voice trembling. "I'll never forgive him."

One piece of evidence caught my attention: a torn piece of fabric near the crime scene. Further analysis revealed it came from a bespoke suit, likely tailored. I discovered that Sophia had recently commissioned a custom suit from a local tailor, and the fabric matched.

Confronting Sophia, I noticed a crack in her composure. She confessed to being at the scene but claimed she didn't commit the crime. But I sensed she was hiding something.

The cryptic notes and recording led me to an old associate of Henry's, who revealed a shocking truth: Henry had been planning to expose a dark secret from Catherine's past, which could ruin the family's reputation. According to the associate, Catherine had been involved in a scandalous affair years ago, and Henry had been using this information to manipulate her.

I realized that Catherine's motive for the murder might be more complex than I initially thought. I decided to investigate her alibi further and discovered a discrepancy in her story. Further investigation revealed she had a hidden safe in her room, containing a gun that matched the one used in the murder.

But just as I thought I had my killer, new evidence emerged: a security camera caught Alex arguing with his father near the study on the night of the murder. The footage showed Alex's shirt sleeve torn, matching the fabric found at the scene.

I was torn between two suspects, each with a motive and opportunity. That's when I realized the true complexity of the case. I decided to bring Alex and Sophia in for further questioning, hoping to crack the case wide open.

As I questioned them, I noticed something peculiar. Both Alex and Sophia seemed to be hiding something, but not in the way I expected. It was as if they were protecting each other, or perhaps themselves.

It felt as if there was a plot twist to this case and of course there was one. Each case has a plot twist, it points to one person, then another and keeps changing directions. That's what is so intriguing about these murder cases; everyone is a suspect and you never know who's the killer.

Alex and Sophia were both being manipulated by Catherine. She had used their own secrets against them, making it seem like one of them had committed the crime. The torn fabric and bespoke suit were red herrings, intentionally planted to mislead the investigation.

The true killer? Catherine, the seemingly composed wife. She had planned the murder meticulously, using her knowledge of the family's dynamics to her advantage. The cryptic notes and recording were part of her plan, designed to frame one of her family members for the crime.

Catherine's motive? Protecting her own dark past, which Henry had discovered. She would stop at nothing to keep her secrets buried, even if it meant killing her husband.

As I confronted Catherine with the evidence, her composure finally cracked. "You'll never understand," she said, her voice cold and calculating. "I did what I had to do to protect my family."

But protect them from what? The truth, it turned out, was far more sinister. Catherine's past was marked by a tragic event, one that could ruin her family's reputation if exposed. Henry had discovered this secret and was using it to control her. Catherine's actions, though misguided, were a desperate attempt to protect her family from the consequences of her past.

Justice was served, but the true horror lay in the depths of human depravity. The case closed, but the experience left me shaken. I'd uncovered the truth, but at what cost? The darkness I'd glimpsed would haunt me forever.

Detective Jameson called me in for an investigation with Catherine. He told me that Catherine wasn't answering any of his questions. He assumed I could try and get through to her, so I agreed.

As I sat across from Catherine in the dimly lit interrogation room, the weight of her secrets hung in the air like a challenge. The case was all but closed, but I couldn't shake the feeling that there was more to Catherine's story.

"So, Catherine," I began, my voice measured, "we've pieced together the events leading up to Henry's murder. But I think there's more to your story than you're letting on."

Catherine's eyes narrowed slightly, a hint of wariness creeping into her expression. "What do you mean?"

"I mean," I continued, leaning forward slightly, "your past. The secret Henry was blackmailing you over. What was it?"

Catherine's gaze dropped, and for a moment, I thought she'd refuse to answer. But then, with a deep breath, she began to speak.

"It's not what you think," she said, her voice low and guarded. "I'm not just a victim of circumstance. I'm...I'm not who you think I am."

I leaned back in my chair, intrigued. "Go on."

Catherine's eyes locked onto mine, a mix of fear and determination in her gaze. "My real name isn't Catherine Richardson. It's Catherine Harrington. I'm the daughter of a notorious con artist. Growing up, I was taught how to manipulate people, how to play the game. And I became good at it. I married Henry for his wealth and status, but also to escape my past."

She paused, collecting her thoughts before continuing.

"But Henry discovered my true identity and threatened to expose me. He used it to control me, to make me do his bidding. I was trapped, and I felt like I had no way out."

Catherine's voice cracked, and for a moment, I saw a glimmer of vulnerability beneath her composed exterior.

"I know it doesn't excuse what I did," she said, her voice barely above a whisper. "But I hope you can understand why I felt like I had no other choice."

As I listened to Catherine's revelation, I felt a complex mix of emotions. Sympathy for her situation, perhaps, but also a deep sense of unease. The woman sitting across from me was a master manipulator, and I couldn't help but wonder how much of her story was true.

The investigation was over, but the truth about Catherine Harrington, aka Catherine Richardson, would stay with me forever, a reminder of the complexities of human nature.

TWELVE

OPPONENTS TO TEAM PLAYERS

I stood outside the school auditorium, my heart racing with excitement and nerves. The annual student council election was just around the corner, and I had thrown my hat into the ring. My platform focused on improving school facilities and increasing student involvement in decision-making.

As I walked into the auditorium, I saw my opponent, Tyler, confidently shaking hands with students. His campaign posters plastered the walls, showcasing his bright smile and catchy slogans. I felt a surge of determination. This was going to be a tough competition.

The debate was intense. Tyler emphasized school spirit and tradition, while I highlighted my experience in student organizations. I spoke passionately about the need for change and the importance of listening to students' voices. Tyler countered with his own vision, and the audience listened intently.

After the debate, I campaigned tirelessly, talking to students, and handing out flyers. My team worked alongside me; their enthusiasm infectious. We brainstormed ideas, planned events, and strategized our next moves.

Election Day had finally arrived, and nerves buzzed through me like electricity. I could barely sit still, glancing at the clock every few minutes, waiting for the moment that would define everything I had worked for. Around campus, my friends and family showed up in full force, proudly wearing "Maya for President" buttons and chanting my name with unstoppable energy. The support was overwhelming—it wrapped around me like a warm embrace, reminding me why I had stepped up to run in the first place.

As the ballots were counted, time seemed to slow. The silence in the room was deafening. I held my breath, hands clenched, heart thudding in my chest. Then, finally, the results were announced—I had won. I had actually won. A wave of emotion crashed over me—relief, joy, gratitude—and I felt tears prick my eyes as applause erupted all around.

I stepped up to the microphone, trying to steady my voice, and looked out at the crowd that had believed in me every step of the way. "Thank you," I began, my voice shaking with feeling. "Thank you for trusting me, for standing with me, and for believing in what we can accomplish together." I promised then and there to give everything I had—to listen, to lead, and to work tirelessly for every single student. This victory wasn't just mine—it was ours.

As I took office, I realized that the real challenge lay ahead. I vowed to listen to my peers, work collaboratively with the administration, and make meaningful changes. The school's future looked brighter with me at the helm.

But little did I know, my biggest test was yet to come. A group of students approached me with concerns about the school's budget cuts. They felt their voices weren't being heard, and they wanted me to do something about it. I listened intently, taking notes and asking questions. I knew I had to act fast to regain their trust and prove that I was a leader who truly cared.

I decided to organize a town hall meeting, where students could share their concerns and ideas. I worked with the administration to ensure that their voices were heard. The meeting was a huge success, and students felt empowered to make a difference.

As I looked out at the crowd of enthusiastic students, I knew that I had made the right decision. Being a leader wasn't just about winning an election; it was about serving others and making a positive impact. I was determined to continue working hard and making a difference in our school community.

The days turned into weeks, and the weeks turned into months. I worked tirelessly to address the concerns of the students. I met with the administration, brainstormed solutions, and implemented changes. And slowly but surely, our school began to transform.

Students began to walk the halls with a new kind of confidence. Their ideas were no longer ignored—they sparked change. Voices that once felt small were now shaping real decisions. School felt different: brighter, more alive. The shift wasn't just physical—it was in the air. There was laughter, collaboration, pride. And in the middle of it all, I stood proud, not because I had done it alone, but because we had done it—together.

Looking back on the journey, I realized something powerful: leadership isn't about the title or the spotlight. It's about the people you lift up along the way. I had discovered strength I didn't know I had, and learned that change doesn't come from shouting the loudest—it comes from listening the hardest. I had grown—not just as a student, but as a person.

But as time went on, the pressure started to build. The meetings piled up, the expectations grew heavier, and the energy I once had began to waver. Balancing everything—schoolwork, leadership, friendships—became a daily challenge. There were moments I felt like I was barely keeping up, moments I questioned whether I could do it all. But deep down, I knew one thing for sure: I wasn't ready to give up. Not now.

I sat in my office, surrounded by stacks of paperwork and enthusiastic students. We had been brainstorming ideas for weeks, and the list of demands was growing. Many students wanted air conditioners installed in the school, a new music room, and a dance room. Others wanted to revamp the library, making it a more inviting and modern space.

The library renovation was a top priority. Students wanted to reorganize the shelves, add comfortable seating areas, and decorate the walls with inspiring quotes and artwork. They envisioned a space where they could relax, study, and explore their creativity.

However, getting the student council to agree on these proposals was proving to be a challenge. Some members were hesitant, citing budget constraints and logistical issues. I knew we needed a solid plan to make these changes a reality.

As I pondered our next move, an idea struck me. Why not reach out to Tyler, my opponent in the election? He had shown himself to be charismatic and resourceful. Perhaps his skills could be put to use in helping us achieve our goals.

I took a deep breath and picked up the phone. "Hey Tyler, it's Maya. I was thinking...since we're both passionate about improving our school, maybe we could work together on some projects."

Tyler's voice was warm and friendly on the other end of the line. "I'd love to help, Maya. What's on your mind?"

"Well," I began, "we've been discussing some big changes – ACs, a music room, a dance room, and a library renovation. But we're having trouble getting everyone on the same page. I was thinking, since you have some great ideas and connections, maybe you could join our team and help us make it happen."

There was a pause, and then Tyler said, "You know what? I think I can do that. I'm in. When do we start?"

A smile spread across my face. This could be the start of something amazing. "How about we meet tomorrow afternoon? We can discuss the details and come up with a plan."

"Sounds like a plan," Tyler agreed. "I'll be there."

As I hung up the phone, I felt a surge of excitement. With Tyler on board, we might just be able to make our vision for the school a reality. The future looked bright, and I couldn't wait to see what we could achieve together.

Over the next few days, Tyler and I worked tirelessly to bring our vision to life. We met with students, teachers, and administrators, gathering feedback and brainstorming solutions.

Some of the things we did included:

- Conducting surveys to gauge student interest in the proposed projects

- Meeting with the school administration to discuss budget allocations and feasibility
- Collaborating with the facilities team to design the new music room and dance room
- Brainstorming ideas for the library renovation, including comfortable seating areas and interactive displays
- Reaching out to local businesses and organizations to secure sponsorships and donations

As we worked together, Tyler's skills and connections proved invaluable. He brought a fresh perspective and creative ideas to the table, and his experience in campaigning helped us navigate the complexities of school politics.

I was impressed by Tyler's dedication and work ethic. Despite our initial rivalry, we quickly fell into a productive rhythm, bouncing ideas off each other and building on each other's strengths.

Together, we presented our proposals to the student council, and to our delight, they were met with enthusiasm. The council members were impressed by our thorough research and creative solutions, and we were able to secure the necessary funding and support for our projects.

As the days turned into weeks, our hard work began to pay off. The school started to transform, with new facilities and programs taking shape. Students were excited to see the changes, and the atmosphere was electric with anticipation.

The library renovation was one of the first projects to be completed. We had added comfortable seating areas, interactive displays, and inspiring quotes on the walls. The space was buzzing with students, who were enjoying the new amenities and discovering new interests.

The music room and dance room were also taking shape. We had secured state-of-the-art equipment and instruments, and students were already starting to use the facilities. The sound of music and laughter filled the air, and it was clear that these rooms would become hubs of creativity and self-expression.

As for the ACs, we were still working on securing the necessary funding. But with Tyler's help, we were confident that we could make it happen. We had already started brainstorming ideas for fundraising events and campaigns, and we were determined to make our school a cooler and more comfortable place to learn.

Overall, our collaboration had been a huge success. We had achieved so much in a short amount of time, and the school was starting to reflect our vision. I was proud of what we had accomplished.

As I looked around at the transformed school, I couldn't help but think about the journey that had brought us here. Tyler and I had started out as rivals, each with our own vision for the school. But through our shared passion for improvement, we had discovered a common goal and worked together to achieve it.

Our initial rivalry had given way to a strong partnership, and eventually, a genuine friendship. We had learned to appreciate each other's strengths and weaknesses, and our differences had become the foundation of a powerful collaboration.

As I glanced over at Tyler, who was chatting with a group of students, I felt a sense of gratitude and admiration. We had come a long way from our election rivalry.

Our story was a testament to the power of collaboration and friendship. Even those who may have started out as rivals or opponents could find common ground and work towards a shared goal.

As we walked out of the school building, Tyler turned to me and smiled. "You know, I never thought I'd say this, but I'm glad we ran against each other in that election."

I smiled back, nodding in agreement. "Me too. Who knows what would have happened if we hadn't?"

Tyler chuckled. "Maybe nothing would have changed, and we'd still be stuck with the same old school."

I laughed. "But instead, we made something happen. We made a difference."

And as we walked off into the sunset, I knew that our friendship and partnership would continue to drive positive change in our school community for years to come.

THIRTEEN

PLAN B- A TWIST IN FATE

I sat on the couch, watching my sister Bailey pace back and forth in our living room, her eyes fixed on the sheet of paper in her hand. She was muttering to herself, trying to memorize the lyrics to "Love Me Like You Do," the song she would be singing at her school's annual concert. Our Performing Arts International School was known for its rigorous curriculum and talented students, and Bailey was determined to shine on stage.

Just then, the doorbell rang, and Bailey's friend Chase walked in. He was also a student at the school and would be performing alongside Bailey in the concert. They would be dancing to "Middle of the Night" and Chase would be playing the guitar while Bailey sang "Love Me Like You Do."

"Hey, guys!" Chase said, dropping his backpack on the floor. "Ready to practice?"

Bailey nodded enthusiastically, and Chase began to set up his guitar. I watched as he expertly tuned the strings and started playing the opening chords to "Middle of the Night."

Bailey took a deep breath and began to dance, her movements fluid and precise. Chase joined in, playing the guitar and singing along to the lyrics. I watched, mesmerized, as they glided across the room, their movements perfectly in sync.

As they practiced, Chase provided feedback and guidance, helping Bailey perfect her dance moves. I sat on the couch, taking note of every step, every gesture, and every smile. Bailey was determined to nail the choreography, and Chase was happy to help her.

After a few run-throughs of the dance, Chase put down his guitar and sat next to me on the couch. "Okay, now let's work on the song," he said, pulling out a sheet of lyrics. "Bailey, you need to practice your vocals."

Bailey nodded, taking a deep breath. "Okay, let's do this."

Chase began to play the guitar again, this time accompanying Bailey as she sang "Love Me Like You Do." Her voice was strong and clear, and I could see the passion and emotion she poured into every word.

As they practiced, I sat there, observing and learning. I was impressed by Bailey's dedication and Chase's expertise. They were both incredibly talented, and I knew they would knock it out of the park at the concert.

After a few hours of practice, Bailey and Chase took a break, sitting down on the couch beside me. "How's it going?" Chase asked, grinning.

Bailey smiled, looking relieved. "I think I'm getting it. Thanks for helping me, Chase."

Chase nodded. "No problem, happy to help. We're going to crush it at the concert."

I nodded in agreement, feeling proud of my sister and her friend. They were going to do amazing things, and I couldn't wait to see them shine on stage.

As Bailey and Chase continued to practice, they decided it was time to call over the rest of the dancers to join in. Bailey pulled out her phone and sent out a group text, inviting everyone to come over to our house for a full group practice.

Before long, the living room was filled with energetic chatter and laughter as the other dancers arrived. I watched as they all gathered around Bailey and Chase, eager to run through the choreography for "Middle of the Night" together.

To my surprise, Bailey asked me if I'd like to join in on the practice too. I wasn't a student at their school, but I'd always loved dancing and had even taken a few classes on the side. I hesitated for a moment, but Bailey encouraged me to give it a try.

Before I knew it, I was dancing along with the group, trying my best to keep up with the intricate steps and movements. Chase played the guitar, and Bailey sang along, guiding the group through the choreography.

It was exhilarating to be a part of the group, even if it was just for fun. I felt like I was part of something special, something that brought everyone together. The energy in the room was electric, and I couldn't help but get caught up in the excitement.

As we practiced, Bailey and Chase provided feedback and guidance, helping everyone perfect their movements. I was impressed by their leadership skills and their passion for dance.

After a few hours of practice, we all took a break, sitting down on the couch and floor, exhausted but exhilarated. "This is going to be epic!" one of the dancers exclaimed.

Bailey grinned, looking happy and relieved. "I know, right? We're going to rock that stage!"

Then came the day of the concert. Everyone sitting in the audience enjoying the show and all the students giving it their best.

As the lights dimmed and the curtains opened, signalling the start of the grand finale, I was sitting in the audience with my parents, eagerly waiting to see Bailey shine on stage. But before the performance could begin, the principal approached us and called us backstage. My heart sank as I saw the look of concern on his face.

"I'm afraid Bailey's been injured," he said, his voice laced with worry. "She tripped on a costume hanger while practicing and broke her arm. She's been rushed to the hospital."

My parents and I exchanged worried glances. What would happen to the concert now? The grand finale was just moments away, and they couldn't cancel it.

That's when Chase stepped forward, his eyes shining with determination. "Hailey knows the choreography and the lyrics," he said. "She can do both, the dance and the song. She's been practicing with us."

The principal looked at me uncertainly, but Chase's confidence was infectious. "Let's do it," he said finally. "Hailey, you're on."

My heart racing, I nodded and followed Chase to the stage. As the music began, I felt a rush of adrenaline coursing through my veins. I took a deep breath and let the music take over.

The spotlight shone down on me, and I felt like I was in my element. I danced with every fiber of my being, my movements precise. Chase played the guitar, and I sang "Love Me Like You Do" with all my heart. The crowd erupted into cheers and applause as I twirled and spun across the stage, feeling like a true performer.

As I reached the climax of the song, I felt a sense of freedom and joy that I'd never experienced before. I was lost in the moment, and everything else faded away. The music, the lights, the crowd – it all came together in a perfect harmony.

When the song ended, the audience erupted into applause, cheering and whistling. I took a bow, grinning from ear to ear, feeling like I'd just accomplished something incredible. Chase smiled at me, and I knew we'd done it together.

As I left the stage, I felt a sense of pride and accomplishment. I'd never expected to be thrust into the spotlight like that, but I'd risen to the challenge. And in that moment, I knew that I'd found something special – a love for performing, and a sense of confidence that would stay with me forever.

When I went backstage, all of the students were smiling and waiting for me and Chase. Everyone congratulated each other. Many students came up to me and said it was amazing how I handled everything last minute.

The principal approached me with a warm smile. "Hailey, I must say, you were absolutely fantastic out there," he said. "Your talent and poise on stage are truly impressive. I'd like to offer you admission to our school, effective immediately. We believe you have a great future in the performing arts, and we'd be honoured to help you develop your skills."

I was taken aback, but the thought of joining Bailey and Chase, and being part of such a talented community, was thrilling. I nodded eagerly, and the principal extended his hand, sealing the deal. I couldn't wait to see what the future held, and I knew that this was just the beginning of an incredible journey.

FOURTEEN

THE OTHER HALF OF ME

I had a geography project due today, which I didn't remember to complete until last night. I was working all night on it causing me to barely pay attention in class. Every class I went to, I was just thinking if my project would be good enough to get an A+.

Then came geography class, I couldn't even bring myself to open my eyes until Ms. Stevenson mentioned that the project has been postponed as we have a new student in our class.

I really hate it when stuff like this happens. I worked all night, so much that my brain could barely process anything anymore. Then came along a new kid, because of whom I have to present the project next week.

All of my hard work went to waste, but at least I don't have to stress anymore. I could re-do the whole thing and it would be much better than what I made out of literal scraps last night.

Finally, I stopped daydreaming and decided to see what the new student looked like. It was a boy about my height with brown eyes and jet-black hair. He wore glasses which I thought looked cool.

He seemed really nice, but despite that, the rest of my friends just bullied him the entire class. I felt absolutely horrible for how my friends treated him. Its already difficult for him to fit in, bullying him will just make him feel worse.

My friend group has this one rule- no matter how nice a person may be, we won't let them into our trio. I honestly don't think it's a great idea. We're a few of the popular kids in school.

My friends think the whole world revolves around them, while I'm the kind one of the group. They say that new kids are a nuisance and that they don't deserve to be a part of the school. I don't understand their logic because I was once a new kid too, yet they let me into their group.

They encourage me to bully new students and not talk to them other insulting them but I know that's never going to happen.

I signal my friends multiple times to cut it out and leave him alone. But no matter how many times I told them to stop, they wouldn't listen.

I know what it feels like to be the new kid, to have trouble making friends, to catch up with all the previous work and to fit in. My friends, on the other hand, don't understand this and never could. They've been in this school their whole lives and have known each other since.

After class, I ran out of the classroom to catch up with my friends. I looked at them with eyes full of disappointment until Tina asked, "What?".

I tell them to think how they would react if they were in his place. Tom says, "I wouldn't be a cry-baby like him. I would suck it up and deal with it. Plus, why are you standing up for him? You're like the most popular girl in school."

I'm left astonished. The people I trusted with my lives, with everything turned out to be bullies. Years ago, I thought they were just going through a disturbing phase of life that caused them to be like this, but now I realise that they're the exact opposite of me.

I wanted to help others and make the world a better place for everyone. My friends; they only care about themselves and just want everybody to deal with their own problems.

I just stand there staring at them in shock. I finally speak up, "What is wrong with you guys? How could you do this? He's a person just like us and now he's in this school, so doesn't he deserve to be a part of it?"

My friends brushed it off and headed to their next class. They even had the audacity to tell me I was overreacting.

The rest of the day I could only think about how that new kid must be feeling. He was literally too shy to introduce himself; he didn't even tell the class his name.

At lunch, my friends call me over to our usual table. I roll my eyes yet still go. Tina says, "C'mon Lilac. Sit with us, it's like you've been avoiding us the whole day. What's going on?"

I sigh and slightly laugh. "Wow!", I say sarcastically. "You very well know what's going on. By the way, I am avoiding you guys. I don't even feel like being around you anymore. If you're going to treat innocent students horribly like bullies, this friendship is over. You can find someone else to join your gang."

I see the new boy at lunch. I remembered the rule my friends told me- NEVER TALK TO NEW KIDS. But then I realised, I just left my old friends so why should I still follow their rules.

At first, I doubt myself but then approach him and ask if I could sit with him. He agrees and recalls that we were in the same class just this morning.

I smile and tell him that I noticed him too. I also apologized for my friends' behaviour towards him. He reassures me that its completely ok and that he goes through bullying a lot.

The vibe I was getting changes from a happy tone to a bit depressing one. I softly say, "I'm sorry you had to go through all that. We haven't formally met. My name's Lilac. Why are you smiling?"

He smiles and replies, "It's not illegal to smile, I can smile if I want to." That made me blush hard. He continued, "oh yeah, my name is James Monet."

The bell rang and we headed to class. We talked a lot for one day. I was hoping we would become better friends in the future.

The next time I meet James, it was kind of unexpected. I was sitting on the grass near the lake behind the school, sketching the trees like I always do after class, when he walked over and asked if he could sit.

He was holding a book—Allies by Alan Gratz, I remember—and he asked what I was drawing. That was the start. We ended up talking for over an hour, about books, music, and why the sky looks different at dusk. I eventually even told him about the geography project.

When he left, he said, "Same time tomorrow?" I just nodded, surprised but curious.

After that, we started meeting at the lake almost every afternoon. Sometimes he brought snacks; once he even brought these terrible peanut butter crackers that crumbled into dust in our hands; and I always brought my sketchbook. He didn't draw, but he liked watching me.

"You see things differently," he said once. It made me self-conscious, but also strangely proud. We'd talk about anything and everything. His old school. My love for thunderstorms. How quiet the lake got when the sun started to set. We didn't need a plan; we just kept showing up.

One Saturday, he texted me and asked if I wanted to go to the art museum downtown. I didn't even know he had my number.

We met outside the museum; he was wearing this grey hoodie that looked like it had been through a few too many washes. We wandered through the galleries, pointing out our favourite paintings.

He liked modern abstract stuff; I leaned toward anything moody and old. He teased me about it, said I had a "Victorian ghost energy," whatever that meant. We got coffee afterwards and sat on a bench watching people go by. That day felt like something more.

As the weeks went on, our meetups got more frequent and less formal. Once, he helped me build a cardboard sculpture for my art project, even though he claimed he had zero creative talent.

We spent the whole afternoon in my garage with glue guns and tape, music playing from his phone. He got more glue on himself than the project, but I laughed so hard I didn't care.

Another time, I helped him study for a math quiz. He was terrible at math, but it was mostly an excuse to hang out again. We ended up watching Mr. Beast on his laptop instead.

One rainy evening, I texted him asking if he wanted to walk in the rain with me. I thought he'd say no, but he showed up with two mismatched umbrellas—one blue, one clear—and a ridiculous grin. We walked through the park while the rain soaked our shoes, talking about nothing and everything.

At one point, he told me that meeting me had made this new town feel like home. I didn't say anything, but I felt it too. It was strange how normal he felt, how easy it had become to just be around him.

Our hangouts became something I looked forward to, not just because they were fun, but because they made life feel lighter. Whether we were sitting on the roof of the old gym at night watching stars or grabbing fries from that sketchy diner near Main Street.

It was like every moment carved out its own memory. He started showing up at my art exhibits, even if they were small school ones. And I started walking home with him more often, even if it meant a longer route. We never really defined what we were, but we didn't need to.

Then one day, James just... disappeared. No warning. No message. One morning he was there, walking beside me through the school gates like always, and by the next, he was gone. His phone was off. His room untouched. His parents were frantic, but the police found nothing.

Days blurred into weeks. I kept going to the lake after school, half-hoping he'd be there waiting with some sarcastic comment or one of those terrible snacks he liked. But he never showed.

A few months after he vanished, his parents called me over. I hadn't seen them since the incident. They looked tired in a way that no sleep could fix. They handed me a pair of old black headphones in a worn-out cloth pouch.

"He left these for you," his mom said, her voice quiet and trembling. "Said you'd know when to use them." I took them, not knowing what to do with them, only that I couldn't let them go.

I didn't listen. Not then. It felt too raw, too unreal. So I tucked them away in a box under my bed, alongside my sketchbooks and every drawing I'd ever made of him.

Two years passed. The ache dulled but never left. Every now and then I'd dream of him—his laugh, the way he leaned back when he was thinking, the way he said my name like it meant something.

The day before what would've been his birthday, I found myself rummaging through that old box. My fingers brushed against the headphones, and before I could talk myself out of it, I put them on. My hands were shaking. I didn't even notice the tiny recorder built into the side until it clicked on with a soft beep.

His voice came through, a little crackly, but unmistakably James. "I smiled that day at lunch, the first time we met," he began, "because I recalled my mom telling me I have a long-lost sister named Lilac."

I stopped breathing. "When I found out we had the same last name, and that you were adopted... I knew it was you. I didn't know how to tell you. I didn't want to scare you. But I knew. I've always known. And being around you felt like coming home. So now that you know, trust me. I will come back to you."

I sat frozen, the world spinning around me. Everything we'd shared, everything he'd said—those quiet glances, the way he always asked about my childhood, how he never once mentioned his own in detail—it all started clicking into place.

The next morning when I woke up, it felt rather strange. Different from how it usually was. I still couldn't believe that my best friend was my brother. I told my parents and they said that if I ever felt like I wanted to move in with James' parents; my biological parents, I could.

They were so supportive of the situation knowing how much this meant to me. I loved my adoptive parents a lot. But in this case, I had to be with my birth family, James' family. I owe it to James for always being there for me.

Just as I ran down the street to James' house to tell his parents, I felt as if James was running beside me holding my hand. I started crying, I couldn't hold it in any longer.

When I reached James' house. His mom saw me crying and called me inside. She was worried for me as if I was her own child; which I was. She asked what happened. Before I could even start, James walked down the stair case and asked, "What's wrong sis?"

I ran and gave him a big hug. I asked, "Why didn't you tell me? James, I would have believed you no matter what."

His father replied, "We knew too, kiddo. James wanted to tell you desperately but we stopped him. The time wasn't right, we were worried it would interfere with both of your studies."

I understood why they didn't tell me. They were worried about how it would affect me. I asked them when James came back?

James said, "I'll tell you myself. I was kidnapped. I didn't even realise it was 2 years. But when you put on the headphones, I just sensed you, I felt you. I knew I had to come back. So, I fought as hard as I could and came back yesterday night covered in blood. I even climbed through your room window before coming home. I had to make sure you were safe. And now that you know, we can make it official to the school, to everyone. You're always free to come live here if you want."

The words barely came out of my mouth, "Thank you. Happy Birthday." I shifted in with them a couple of days after.

Even at my graduation party, during my speech I said, "To my best friend, to my brother, to James." Let's just say my old friends Tina and Tom did not take that very well.

Till this day, James and I are the only people who know that we became friends because I owed it to him for postponing that geography project.

FIFTEEN

THE THREAD OF TIME

I stumbled upon an old watchmaker's shop. The sign creaked in the wind, reading "Timekeeper's Delight." I pushed open the door, and a bell above it rang out. The shop was dimly lit, filled with the scent of old leather and oil. Behind the counter stood an old man with spectacles perched on the end of his nose.

"Welcome, young one," he said, his voice dripping with mystery. "I've been expecting you."

He handed me a peculiar watch with intricate engravings. "This is a timekeeper," he explained. "It will take you to any moment in history, in certain cases the future. But be warned: the consequences of your actions can be unpredictable."

I was sceptical, but curiosity got the better of me. I wound the watch, set the dials, and pressed the button.

The world around me blurred, and I felt a strange sensation, like being pulled apart and put back together. When my vision cleared, I found myself standing in the middle of a bustling street in ancient Egypt.

I wandered through the markets, marvelling at the pyramids and the vibrant culture. But as I watched a group of workers constructing a massive stone structure, I noticed a young pharaoh watching from the shadows. Our eyes met, and he nodded in recognition.

Suddenly, I realized I had a chance to change the course of history. I approached the pharaoh and whispered a suggestion that would alter the fate of his kingdom. As I returned to my own time, I felt a thrill of excitement.

But when I opened my eyes, I found myself in a world unlike any I had known. Skyscrapers lay in ruins, and people dressed in clothing as if scavenging for food. A news headline caught my eye: "Global Collapse: Ancient Egyptian Empire's Descendants Rule the World."

I realized the timekeeper's warning was not just a cautionary tale. My actions had created a completely different future.

Determined to find a way to restore the timeline, I decided to look into the future. I wound the new watch, set the dials to a future date, and pressed the button. The familiar sensation washed over me, and I felt myself being pulled through time.

When my vision cleared, I found myself standing in a futuristic city. Towering buildings made of materials I had never seen before stretched towards the sky. Flying cars zipped by, and people of all ages walked by with augmented reality glasses.

I wandered through the city, marvelling at the advancements. But as I walked, I noticed a group of people gathered around a large screen displaying a news headline: "Timeline Restoration Project: Scientists Discover Way to Fix Anomalies."

My heart skipped a beat. Could this be the solution? I pushed my way through the crowd and approached one of the scientists. "Excuse me," I said, trying to sound calm. "Can you tell me more about this project?"

The scientist looked at me with curiosity. "We're working on a way to repair anomalies in the timeline. We've detected a rogue time traveller who altered the course of history, causing significant disruptions."

I felt a shiver run down my spine. They were talking about me. "Do you know who the time traveller is?" I asked, trying to sound nonchalant.

The scientist hesitated. "We're still trying to identify them. But we have reason to believe they're still jumping through time, trying to fix their mistakes."

I realized that I had to be careful. If the scientists discovered my identity, they might try to stop me. But I also felt a glimmer of hope. Maybe, just maybe, I could work with them to restore the timeline.

As I stood there, pondering my next move, the watch on my wrist seemed to pulse with energy. I knew that I had to tread carefully, but I was determined to set things right.

I decided to approach the scientist further, trying to gather more information without revealing my true identity. "What's the plan to fix the timeline?" I asked, trying to sound genuinely interested.

The scientist nodded, launching into a detailed explanation of their research. "We're developing a technology that can pinpoint the exact moment where the timeline was altered. Once we identify the anomaly, we can send a temporal agent to correct it."

I listened intently, my mind racing with possibilities. If I could get access to this technology, maybe I could use it to fix the timeline myself.

As I continued to chat with the scientist, I noticed a figure watching us from across the room. They seemed out of place among the futuristic crowd, dressed in attire that looked almost... ancient.

The figure caught my eye and nodded subtly. I felt a shiver run down my spine. Who was this person, and how did they know me?

The scientist noticed my distraction and followed my gaze. "Ah, that's Dr. Amentop. He's a historian who's been helping us understand the ancient Egyptian empire's influence on modern society."

Dr. Amentop. The name sounded familiar. Suddenly, it clicked – he was the pharaoh I had advised in ancient Egypt. What was he doing here?

As I pondered this question, Dr. Amentop approached us. "Ah, you're interested in the timeline restoration project?" he asked, his eyes piercing.

I nodded, trying to play it cool. "Yes, I'm just curious about the technology."

Dr. Amentop smiled. "I think we could use someone with your... unique perspective. Would you like to join our team?"

My heart skipped a beat. Join the team? What did he know about me? I hesitated, unsure of what to do next.

The watch on my wrist seemed to be pulsing faster now, as if urging me to make a decision. What could I possibly do?

I thought about what would happen if they found it was me who was their unidentified time traveller. But if I do join their team, I would figure out a lot about how to make things right.

I turned around for a moment and suddenly bumped into someone. I recognized them. It was my best friend.

She exclaimed, "Trixy! Its so nice to see you. Its been so long. I thought you moved to Austin, I wasn't expecting to see you here in Georgia so soon."

I chuckled and said, "I guess you never realise how fast time flies. Isn't that right, Jess?" She smiled back at me and offered to let me stay with her for a couple of days.

I was grateful for it too. The scientists asked if I had made up my mind. The second Dr. Amentop asked me that, Jess pulled me to a corner and told me that these guys act like they're figuring it out but in reality, they have no idea what they're doing.

She even told me that she had been in their so-called lab and took pictures of all the resources they've been wasting. She planned to expose them soon, I couldn't believe it.

This was getting too crazy, I longed to return to my own time, to fix the timeline, but the watch was gone.

The old man reappeared, his eyes twinkling. "You see, young one, time travel is a delicate art. The consequences of our actions can be far-reaching."

He handed me a new watch, one that would take me back to my own time. "But remember, the timeline is fragile. Tread carefully."

I set the dials, feeling a mix of relief and doubt. As the world blurred around me once more, I knew that I would never take my own time for granted again.

When I returned to my own world, I felt grateful for a second chance. I vowed to use my knowledge to make a positive impact, rather than altering the course of history. The timekeeper's lesson had taught me the value of appreciating the present.

I looked down at my wrist, where the watch now rested. The engravings seemed to whisper a warning: "Time is fragile. Handle with care."

SIXTEEN

THE SCUBA SURPRISE

I ran towards the bus stop as fast as I could, I didn't notice my dad running after me. Just as I'm about to get on the bus, my dad approaches me and says, "Katie, there's no way I'm letting you go to school on an empty stomach." He hands me a sandwich, "eat this in the bus."

I boarded the bus, took a seat, and began eating my sandwich. A girl said, "excuse me." I hadn't noticed I was sitting so close to her. When I offered to move to another seat, she encouraged me to stay with her.

She introduced herself as Leslie and mentioned that it was her first day at school. I responded, "Welcome to Bright Beacon Academy, Leslie. I'm Katie." We chatted for a bit and discovered we were in the same class. She joked by asking, "So, is being late to the bus stop and having to eat your breakfast on the bus a regular thing for you?" I grinned and kept eating my sandwich.

She questions why I'm just in a hoodie and shorts in such cold winter conditions. I explain that I have basketball practice, which requires us to stay in sports uniform; the most we can do is put on a jacket or something over it. She mentions that she's quite skilled in basketball and was the team captain at her previous school. Being a very sociable person, I give her a flyer for the BB team tryouts happening next week.

As we go to school, I take the chance to introduce her to my buddies. I approach my pals and tell them Leslie is on my bus. Then someone puts their hands over my eyes and says, "Guess who?" I respond in a sing-song voice, "Ian, I know it's you."

Stacy describes Ian as an idiot for doing this practically every day. Leslie requests, "Could I get to know everyone's names, please?" Stacy says, "Hello, I'm Stacy, Katie's BFF. That's my foolish brother Ian, Katie's lover. I'm not sure what she sees in him. This is Annie, and that's Brodie. We have many additional members of our gang; you'll get to know them soon enough." Leslie compliments her for her excellent explanation.

The bell rings, and Mr. Anderson walks in. He sees Leslie and says, "Come here, young lady. Hello, everyone. We have a new student, Leslie Jones. Please be really welcoming to her.

Once class has ended, Mr. Anderson brings Leslie to his desk and says softly, "Leslie, you'll need to catch up on all of the work and take a tour of the school. There is a lot of work to be done, so I will assign you a welcome buddy to assist you.

I roll my eyes, approach both of them, and say, "Sir, I appreciate your efforts to help her fit in, but my group and I have already embraced her; we are now her buddies. If we aided with that, we can assist with the remainder. Come on, Leslie."

He becomes irritated and says, "Ms. Miller, it's the first day back to school." Try not to irritate me with your hijinks for once." I chuckle as I walk out the door with Leslie.

During the break, we hurried to the basketball court. David, Natalie, and the rest of the group were there, cheering, "Let's go, Leslie!" I picked up the ball and said, "Come on, new girl, let's see what you can do."

Leslie beamed as she dashed across the court, scoring one basket after another and calling out fouls that no one else seemed to notice. After the match, I gave her a high-five and told her she had the right spirit. Brodie confirmed that she had a lot of potential and that she was now a part of Bright Beacon Academy.

5 MONTHS LATER...

Our entire group gathered in my room, eagerly discussing our upcoming trip to Australia. We were set to go scuba diving and snorkeling at the Great Barrier Reef. We would explore the waters off the beaches in Sydney.

The excitement for this school-organized excursion was immense for everyone. After just 2 days, we arrived in Australia. It was stunning, exceeding all our expectations. Now it was time to go scuba diving.

Leslie and I decided to pair up together. The other pairs were Annie and Natalie, Stacy and Ian, and Brodie and David.

As I stood on the boat, the warm sun beating down on my skin, I felt a rush of excitement mixed with a hint of nervousness. Leslie, my dive buddy, gave me a reassuring smile as we prepared to take the plunge.

The moment of truth arrived, and we rolled off the side of the boat, our scuba gear securely fastened to our bodies. The water enveloped me like a cool blanket, and I felt weightless, suspended in a world unlike any other. Leslie and I exchanged a thumbs-up, and we began our descent into the depths.

As we swam deeper, the water pressure increased, and I felt my ears adjust to the change. I equalized the pressure by pinching my nose shut and blowing gently. Leslie watched me, nodding in approval, and we continued our journey downward.

The scenery shifted dramatically as we descended. The surface's blue-green hue gave way to a vibrant coral reef, teeming with life. Schools of fish darted past us, their scales shimmering in the sunlight that filtered down from above. Leslie and I swam side by side, our eyes scanning the reef for hidden treasures.

We spotted a sea turtle lazily munching on seaweed, its shell glistening in the sunlight. Leslie pointed it out, and I grinned behind my mask. We watched in awe as the turtle swam away, its flippers propelling it effortlessly through the water.

As we explored the reef, I felt a sense of freedom and wonder. The ocean was a vast, mysterious world, full of secrets and surprises. Every swim stroke took us deeper into this alien landscape, and I felt like a space explorer, discovering new worlds and marveling at the beauty around me.

Our dive time flew by, and Leslie signaled that it was time to ascend. We slowly made our way up, pausing at safety stops to allow our bodies to adjust to the changing pressure. As we broke through the surface, I felt a sense of exhilaration and accomplishment. We had experienced something truly special, and I knew that this was just the beginning of our scuba diving adventures together.

As we climbed back onto the boat, Leslie turned to me with a huge grin. "That was amazing!" she exclaimed. I nodded in agreement, still trying to process the incredible sights we had seen. The ocean had left me awestruck, and I couldn't wait till our 2nd dive.

I was trembling, not because of the cold water but because I saw something down there. Leslie noticed that I felt off. I told her about how I saw something in the water, it was something not exactly small but not big either. It was very shiny. Leslie believed me, not doubting a single word I said.

She said, "Stacy and Annie don't want to go for a 2nd dive. So, we can take Natalie with us, and Ian can go with the boys. We can make groups of 3 this time because I'm pretty sure Nat and Ian do not want to be diving partners."

I felt so reassured by Leslie's heartfelt words. She continued as I smiled, "If something's bothering you, we'll figure out what it is. From the very first day I joined this school, you helped me face any problems I ever had. You're literally the reason I'm on the BB team. Now, if you're feeling uncomfortable, its my turn to help you."

We informed Natalie about this as well, and she agreed to our plan. When it was time for our second dive, we headed directly towards the gleaming object. I took the lead.

I took them to it. Once we reached, we discovered it to be an old and dusty treasure chest. It was stuck in the sand, covered in dirt and yet it still chose to shine like a diamond.

Taking it out of the sand was quite tough. The chest didn't feel like it was containing anything too heavy but it was held in the sand very tightly. The three of us tried pulling it but it barely moved.

Just as we were starting to lose hope, we spotted the boys swimming close to us. We called them over and showed them the chest. We couldn't communicate underwater but everyone understood what we were trying to tell each other.

Everyone held it, all 6 of us pulled as hard as we could and after a lot of effort, we finally got it out. The confusing part, the chest was extremely light, almost as if it didn't contain anything inside it.

We took it to the surface and kept it on the boat. One by one we all got onto the boat too. As we took off our gear, we explained everything to Stacy and Annie too.

All that remained between us all was one thing: suspense. What could be inside? Did it hold some ancient secrets? Could the chest have some valuable information or was it just a prank? Did it have jewels in it like in the movies?

We would only find out the answer of these questions when we opened it, so that's what we did.

We opened it to find a piece of paper. It read:

"Congratulations students,

This is a note from your principal. if you are reading this, it means you are one of the very few who like to take upon risks. If you accomplished to discover this as a team, the school is very proud of you for your teamwork. We had hidden this chest beforehand so that if you noticed it, that's amazing. But if you did anything about it, you're brave students. If you saw it but left it be, then I'm sorry but you did not earn anything. This was a competition to see who is the most adventurous group of students. Inside the chest is a trophy, this is an award for your bravery. Congratulations and have a great day ahead.

Signed,

Mr. Davis"

We checked out the trophy, it looked awesome. And to be honest, all of us deserved it. We assumed it could have been something dangerous. But it ended up being a test set up for us by the principal.

Time to head to Sydney. Who knows what awaits us next.

SEVENTEEN

BANANA MODE: GAME ON

Okay, I know how this sounds, but I swear—I didn't mean to become a banana. It wasn't like I woke up that morning and said, "Hey, you know what would make my Saturday better? Getting sucked into a video game and turning into a slippery piece of fruit." But sometimes the universe does weird things, and apparently, it had plans for me.

It all started in my room, which smelled faintly of popcorn, old socks, and the kind of stress that comes from failing Level 9 of Fruit Smash Galaxy for the 50th time.

Fruit Smash Galaxy is this ridiculous but addictive video game where you play as fruit battling evil vegetables. It's got everything—jetpack strawberries, sword-wielding apples, pineapples with sunglasses and attitude.

I'd been trying to beat the final stage for days, but my apple avatar kept getting splatted by a giant broccoli boss with laser eyes. So, I decided to try something new. Just for fun, I scrolled through the avatar options.

That's when I saw it: "Banana Mode – UNLOCKED." It was glowing. I didn't remember unlocking it. I didn't even remember seeing it before. But the controller vibrated in my hands, and before I could stop myself, I clicked it.

Big mistake.

The screen flashed yellow, and a weird humming filled the room. At first, I thought it was just the TV glitching, but then light started pouring out of the screen—literal glowing, pixelated light.

My controller sparked, and the air felt thick like jelly. I barely had time to gasp before I was yanked forward—like something grabbed my whole body and pulled me into the screen. The last thing I saw was my poster of a cat in a wizard hat falling off the wall. And then I was gone.

I landed face-first in what smelled like fruit punch and jellybeans. Everything was bright and bouncy. The sky was cotton-candy pink, and giant grapes hung from trees like balloons.

As I sat up, I realized something was very, very wrong. For starters, my arms were yellow. Not just yellow—they were banana yellow. And curved. And slightly squishy. I looked down and nearly screamed.

My entire body was a giant banana. I had gloves on my hands (do bananas even have hands?), cartoon eyes floating in front of my peel, and tiny sneaker-like feet.

"Initializing Banana Avatar," said a robotic voice above me. "Welcome, Player 1."

"Player 1?" I said. Or at least I tried to say. It came out more like, "Plaaarghwuh?!"

I slapped my banana cheeks and blinked hard. No hoodie. No jeans. Just banana me, standing on a platform made of sugar cubes in the middle of a glittering fruit kingdom.

Before I could even think, a loud siren blared from somewhere in the sky. "ALERT! VEGETABLE ATTACK IN

SECTOR 7! DEPLOYING BANANA UNIT."

"What? Wait—what's a banana unit?!" I yelled. But it was too late. A mechanical spoon dropped from the sky and scooped me up like an ice cream topping. I was catapulted across the sky, flipping and spinning until I crashed into a battlefield made of mashed potatoes and jelly.

All around me, fruit warriors were fighting angry vegetables. Strawberries with bazookas were launching seed bombs at marching rows of robotic broccoli. A carrot tank was spinning in circles, firing out sizzling ranch sauce. In the middle of it all, I lay flat on my banana belly, too stunned to move.

"Banana unit!" shouted a tough-looking mango in a bandana. "Get off your peel and help us flank the zucchini line!"

"I don't even know how to move!" I shouted, struggling to stand. My peel kept slipping on the mashed potatoes. The mango groaned. "Rookies..."

And then, accidentally, I activated a move. I didn't mean to, but when I flailed my banana arms in panic, a glowing icon appeared in the air; Slippery Swipe: Activated.

My body spun like a wheel of fortune, and suddenly I was sliding across the battlefield at banana-warp speed, knocking over broccoli soldiers like bowling pins.

The fruit army erupted into cheers. "Banana's got moves!" yelled a blueberry holding a slingshot.

That battle was bananas. (Pun absolutely intended.) I slipped, spun, crashed, and somehow managed to take out three veggie drones and a tomato turret just by being incredibly clumsy.

By the end of it, I was covered in smoothie goo, but apparently, I'd won us the round. I even levelled up and unlocked something called the "Peel of Justice." Whatever that meant.

After the fight, I found myself in a fruit village made entirely of snacks. The buildings were cookie stacks, the roads were made of licorice, and the air smelled like bubblegum.

A tiny kiwi with a jetpack hovered in front of me and introduced himself as Glitchy, my in-game assistant.

"You've been Banana'd," he said cheerfully. "It's rare. Most players never unlock Banana Mode. Welcome to the Fruit Smash Galaxy."

"Thanks," I said. "Now, how do I log out?"

"Oh," Glitchy blinked. "There's no logging out unless you beat the final boss."

"What final boss?"

"The Salad Lord."

I stared at him. "You're kidding."

"Nope!" Glitchy beeped. "Only way out is to defeat the most powerful vegetable in the galaxy—King Caesar Salad, ruler of the Veggie Empire. Real leafy guy. Bit of a crouton addict. Hates bananas."

"Of course he does.", I murmured under my breath.

I had no choice. If I ever wanted to get back to my real room, my real clothes, and my very confused pet hamster, I'd have to play the game. All of it. And that meant building a team. So, I did.

My first recruit was Berry Boom, a raspberry with an attitude and an explosive personality. Literally—she carried fruit grenades in a backpack made of licorice.

Then I found Mango Max, a mellow surfer-type mango who could ride juice waves and do kickflips midair.

Last but not least was Grapezilla, a massive, muscled grape who only said one word: "SQUISH." Together, we became Team Peel. Our slogan? "We may be fruits, but we don't back down."

We battled through insane levels. The Jelly Jungle, where gummy worms tried to eat us. The Spicy Salsa Volcano, where flying chili peppers chased us through molten nacho lava. The Frozen Yogurt Caverns, home to the dreaded Ice Lettuce Yeti.

I got better. Stronger. I unlocked new powers—Peel Shield, Banana Boomerang, Slippery Slipstream. I even learnt how to bounce off walls like a ninja fruit.

Somewhere along the way, I stopped being afraid. I stopped hating being a banana. In fact... I kind of liked it.

But all good things (even slightly squishy ones) must end.

The time came when we reached the gates of Saladonia. A giant floating castle made of celery, radishes, and croutons loomed ahead, guarded by cauliflower robots and laser kale. The final level.

Inside the throne room stood the Salad Lord— King Ceaser Salad, ten feet tall, made of swirling lettuce, glowing red eyes under a broccoli crown. He smelled like balsamic dressing and doom.

"So," he said in a voice like a blender full of doom, "the Banana comes to challenge me?"

"Yup," I said. "And I brought friends."

The final battle was chaos. Veggie guards threw beetroot bombs and tried to trap us in carrot cages. Grapezilla roared and body-slammed a cucumber dragon. Berry Boom planted charges in the radish walls. Mango Max surfed through a tidal wave of guacamole. And me? I slid straight at King Ceaser Salad with my final move: Banana Blast.

BOOM.

Lettuce flew everywhere. Croutons rained from the sky. And when the dust settled, the Salad Lord was no more. In his place floated a glowing crystal—the Logout Gem.

I walked up to it, peeled and bruised, but grinning. "Time to go home," I said. I touched it. Light flashed.

I blinked—and I was back in my room. Same hoodie. Same game controller on the floor. Same cat wizard poster, now slightly crooked. But something was different.

The game was gone. No more Fruit Smash Galaxy icon on my console. Just a golden banana sticker stuck to my desk. I picked it up. It glowed faintly.

Then it whispered: "Slippery Swipe ready."

I don't know what that means. But I keep it close. Just in case the vegetables come back.

EIGHTEEN

SOULMATES AND SUPERPOWERS

Ugh, Monday mornings. Why did the alarm clock have to ring so early? I groggily opened my eyes, the bright light of the morning piercing through my window. I reached over to slap the snooze button, but my hand hesitated, hovering above the clock. Just five more minutes, I pleaded with myself. But the alarm clock seemed to sense my weakness and continued to shriek, piercing my eardrums.

I tossed and turned, feeling the weight of the bed pulling me back down. Why did I set the alarm so early? I could've slept in, just for a little bit longer. But the thought of being late for school propelled me forward, and I finally mustered the energy to sit up.

After what felt like an eternity, I dragged myself out of bed and began my morning routine. I stumbled through getting dressed, brushing my teeth, and grabbing a quick breakfast. As I rushed out the door, I couldn't help but think that this day was already off to a terrible start.

Little did I know, it was about to get a whole lot more interesting.

I burst through the school doors, out of breath and apologizing to my friends for being late. But as I entered the classroom, I noticed something strange. Everyone was buzzing with excitement, whispering to each other and glancing at the front of the room.

Our principal, Mr. Johnson, stood at the podium, a wide grin spreading across his face. "Welcome, students, to a very special day. As part of our school's anniversary celebration, we've been gifted a unique opportunity. Today, each and every one of you will receive a superpower."

The room erupted into cheers and gasps. I couldn't believe what I was hearing. Superpowers? Was this for real?

Mr. Johnson continued, "We've set up a machine in the auditorium that will assign each of you a superpower. It's completely random, so you'll just have to wait and see what you get."

I couldn't contain my excitement as I followed the crowd to the auditorium. What would my superpower be? Would I be able to fly? Turn invisible? Something even more amazing?

As I waited in line, my heart racing with anticipation, I couldn't help but wonder what lay ahead. And then, it was my turn. I stepped into the machine, feeling a strange tingling sensation wash over me.

The machine beeped, and a screen flashed with my superpower: Super Speed. I couldn't believe it. I was going to be fast. Really fast.

What would I do with this newfound power? The possibilities were endless.

I sat back down next to my friends. After everyone was assigned a superpower, Mr. Johnson stepped onto the podium again.

He announced, "Well, it seems we are done with the process but I have to inform you about something quite essential. 2 people will be given the same power, one boy and one girl; all you need to do is just find your match. The person with your matching power will be your soulmate. This is a new law introduced by the government. Once you find your perfect match, both of you will be a dynamic duo. Oh and you will get an app downloaded on your phones called The Superpower Registry, sooner or later today you will get a notification on the app telling you who your soulmate is. Good luck to all of you."

It's a completely non-sensible idea.

I went and sat next to mine and my friends' meet up spot. Our meet up spot is in front of all of our lockers, it's a sofa next to an artificial plant. We meet up there every day. The plant has little heart shaped cherries on it so we call it "The Cherry Tree".

I trudged to the Cherry Tree, my friends already gathered there, looking like they'd rather be anywhere else. I couldn't blame them; the whole superpower and soulmate announcement was ridiculous. Who did the government think they were, deciding that our soulmates would be determined by some power assignment?

As I approached, Rachel turned to me with a scowl. "Can you believe this, Zara? It's like the government thinks they can dictate who we're meant to be with."

I shook my head. "I know, right? It's the stupidest thing I've ever heard. What if I don't like the person I'm matched with? What if they're a total jerk?"

Mike chimed in, "And what if it's someone from a different school? I don't even know anyone outside of our school."

We all shared our frustrations and concerns about the new law. As we stood there, venting about the situation, I couldn't help but wonder what other absurd rules the government would come up with.

Just then, my phone buzzed with a notification from the Superpower Registry. I groaned, feeling a sense of dread. "Guys, I think it's time to find out who my match is."

My friends nodded in agreement, and we all pulled out our phones to check our matches. I hesitated, my heart racing with anticipation and anxiety.

What if my match was someone I didn't get along with? What if they were completely opposite of me?

I took a deep breath and opened the notification. My match's name was...Ethan Thompson.

I frowned, trying to place the name. "Guys, do any of you know an Ethan Thompson?"

Rachel's eyes widened. "Oh, that's the guy from the debate team. He's pretty smart, but also kind of arrogant."

I raised an eyebrow. "Great, just what I need. A know-it-all for a soulmate."

As we all exchanged information about our matches, I couldn't help but feel a sense of unease. This was not how I wanted to find love or a partner. I wanted to get to know someone, to fall for them naturally, not because some machine said we were meant to be.

I looked around at my friends, seeing the same frustration and uncertainty in their eyes. We were all in this together, forced to navigate this bizarre new world of superpowers and predetermined soulmates.

What would happen when we met our matches? Would we even like each other? Only time would tell. But one thing was for sure: I was not going to let some government dictate my love life without a fight.

I stood outside the school, staring at the notification on my phone. Ethan Thompson. I had to meet him. The government had set up a meeting spot for matches, but I wasn't sure I was ready.

As I walked to the designated area, I saw a figure waiting for me. He was tall, with messy brown hair and piercing blue eyes. He smiled as he saw me, and I felt a flutter in my chest.

"Zara, right?" he asked, his voice confident.

I nodded, trying to play it cool. "Yeah, that's me. Ethan Thompson."

We stood there for a moment, awkwardly silent. I didn't know what to say to him. Did we have to make small talk? Discuss our shared superpower?

Ethan broke the silence. "So, super speed, huh? What do you think about this whole soulmate thing?"

I shrugged. "Honestly, I'm not a fan. I don't think the government should decide who we're meant to be with."

Ethan nodded in agreement. "I know what you mean. It's like they're playing matchmaker or something."

We talked for a while, discussing our concerns and frustrations about the new law. It was nice to know that we shared similar views.

As we parted ways, Ethan smiled and said, "Hey, want to grab coffee sometime this week? Maybe we can get to know each other better."

I hesitated for a moment, unsure if I was ready to spend more time with him. But something about his smile put me at ease. "Yeah, sure. That sounds like fun."

As I walked home, I couldn't help but wonder what the future held for Ethan and me. Would we become more than just matches? Only time would tell.

Over the next few days, Ethan and I met up a few times, getting to know each other better. We discovered that we had a lot in common, from our love of books to our passion for social justice.

But despite our growing connection, I couldn't shake off the feeling that this was all too predetermined. Was I truly falling for Ethan, or was it just because the government said we were meant to be?

I decided to talk to my friends about it. Rachel, Mike, and I sat down over lunch, discussing our experiences with our matches.

"I'm really liking my match," Rachel said. "We have so much in common, and he's really sweet."

Mike nodded. "Yeah, my match is pretty cool too. We're both into gaming, and we have a lot of fun together."

I sighed. "I don't know, guys. I'm just not sure if I'm feeling it with Ethan. It's like, I like him, but is it because I'm supposed to?"

Rachel nodded understandingly. "I get what you mean. It's a lot to take in. But maybe you should just give it time and see how things go."

I nodded, taking her advice to heart. Maybe I just needed to relax and enjoy getting to know Ethan better.

As I walked out of school, I saw Ethan waiting for me. He smiled, and my heart skipped a beat. Maybe, just maybe, this whole soulmate thing wouldn't be so bad after all.

I thought a lot about it every day after school. The next day I saw Ethan standing outside the school gate. I felt so confused. We generally just bump into each other, text, or chat over call. Neither of us ever waited except for on the first day of this nonsense.

As I walked out of school, Ethan turned to me with a nervous smile and took my hand, his eyes sparkling with sincerity. "Zara, from the moment I met you, I knew there was something special about you," he said, his voice filled with emotion. "I was wondering if you'd like to be more than just matches... would you like to be my girlfriend?" My heart skipped a beat as I smiled, feeling a rush of excitement and happiness. "Yes, I'd love to," I replied, and Ethan's face lit up with joy as he pulled me into a gentle hug, the world around us melting away.

Guess we did end up as a dynamic duo like Mr. Johson said. Time for us to fight the villains together. As we smiled at each other I asked him, "You and me against the world?" He chuckled and replied, "You and me against the world."

NINETEEN

GREAT POWER = GREAT RESPONSIBILITY

This morning, I woke up with a fluttering in my stomach that wouldn't go away. The sun peeked through my window, casting soft light on my walls, but it did nothing to calm the storm inside me. I stretched under the covers for a few extra seconds, staring at the ceiling, before finally dragging myself out of bed.

Today wasn't just any school day—it was basketball tryouts, and I'd been thinking about them nonstop all week. I threw on my clothes quickly and barely touched my breakfast, my mind racing through drills, shots, and plays. Every bounce of the ball I imagined, echoed louder than the ticking clock in our kitchen.

When I got to school, the hallways were their usual blur of students, but I felt like I was moving in slow motion. Math class was first, and I slumped into my seat trying to steady my breathing. Mr. Carver started explaining something about quadratic equations, but I couldn't even pretend to pay attention.

My notebook was open, but my pencil just hovered in the air. All I could think about was the court, the pressure of performing well, and whether I'd make the team. What if I missed all my shots? What if someone better showed up? I clenched my jaw and tried to focus on numbers, but the sound of sneakers on hardwood filled my head instead.

By the time the bell rang, I shot out of my seat and practically sprinted to the locker room. I changed into my P.E. uniform quickly—navy shorts and a white top with my school's emblem. My hands trembled slightly as I tied my shoes, but I shook it off and headed to the court.

I grabbed a basketball from the rack and began dribbling, each bounce syncing with my heartbeat. The sound of the ball hitting the floor grounded me, and with every layup and free throw I practiced, I felt more like myself again. The nerves were still there, but muscle memory started taking over.

We started our tryout scrimmage, and that's when everything clicked. I was on. Every move I made felt sharp and deliberate. I scored basket after basket, my adrenaline pushing me faster and harder. At one point, I stole the ball mid-pass and raced down the court, shooting a clean three-pointer that swished perfectly through the net. The sound of it was better than music. My teammates whooped and high-fived me, and even Coach gave a rare smile and nod.

Then, Coach called us all together and laid out the jerseys in a neat row. Each one had a matching jacket, crisp and clean with the school's colours—except one. That jacket was different. It had silver trim and bold lettering on the back that said "CAPTAIN." My heart jumped at the sight of it.

One by one, names were called and players stepped forward to get their gear. When Coach finally said "Lexi," I stepped forward, expecting the standard jacket—but instead, he handed me the captain's. For a moment, I couldn't even breathe. I just stared at it in disbelief before finally taking it in my hands, the fabric soft and heavier than I expected, like it carried real weight.

I slipped on the jacket and grinned so wide my cheeks hurt. The rest of the team clapped and smiled at me, and I felt a new kind of energy spark inside me. This wasn't just about making the team anymore—it was about leading it. I was officially the captain, and I wasn't going to let anyone down.

I zipped up the jacket and looked around at the new faces, my teammates. Some were nervous, others excited. And I was ready to guide them. The court suddenly felt like home. That moment sealed it for me—I knew I belonged here, not just as a player, but as a leader.

We took a break for a few minutes. As we were drinking water, Coach Harris announced, "Those who have made the team, congratulations. You will stay for a while longer as we will have a team photo. Those who didn't make the team, I'm sorry but you did your best and that's what matters. You may now leave."

As our break ended and we huddled together for a team photo, I looked around at all of us in our new gear, the air thick with potential. This was just the beginning. I couldn't wait to train with them, push us all to be better, to win games and build something strong. I could still feel the echo of the ball leaving my hands and hitting that perfect shot. If that tryout was the test, now, it was game time.

As I walked back to class from basketball tryouts, I felt a strange mix of exhaustion and excitement. The cool breeze hit my face, and I decided to take off my captain's jacket for a bit—it was way too warm for something that thick.

Holding it in my arms, I kept replaying the moment when Coach announced I made the team. It felt unreal, like everything I had worked for finally meant something. My legs were sore, my shirt stuck to my back, but none of that mattered—I was officially on the team.

For the first time in what felt like forever, I could actually focus in class. I wasn't overthinking my layups or running imaginary plays in my head. Instead, I sat still, took out my notebook, and actually followed what the teacher was saying.

My mind was clear; the pressure was off. Being on the team meant I could finally breathe again. I even caught myself smiling when I remembered the look on everyone's face when I sank that final shot during tryouts.

After a while, I started to feel a chill. I slipped my jacket back on without thinking much of it. That's when something strange happened. I felt this weird buzzing in my head—like when a TV's on in the background but you can't see it.

I brushed it off and tried to ignore it, but the second I closed my eyes to relax, everything changed. A voice popped into my head—clear as day—but no one around me was speaking. It was the kid sitting right in front of me, and I was hearing his thoughts.

I didn't want to freak out, so I opened my eyes again and looked around. No one else seemed to notice anything. Just to test it, I looked over at the kid sitting next to me and slowly shut my eyes.

There it was again—his thoughts, his worries about a math quiz, his lunch, even the girl he liked in third period. I could hear it all, like his brain was a radio and I had just tuned in. I sat there frozen, heart pounding, not sure whether to laugh or panic.

This jacket—it had to be the jacket. Somehow, it gave me the power to read minds. At first, I couldn't believe it. But the more I tried it, the more real it became. It was wild. I mean, how cool is that? I could hear what people were thinking, their secrets, their fears, their crushes. It was awesome.

At lunch, I decided to go tell my best friend Britney that I made the team and not only that but I'm captain. I look all around the cafeteria for her until I see her sitting in a small cramped up space.

I go up to her, "Hey girl! What's up? Guess who's the captain of the team!" She congratulates me and says that its amazing but she doesn't really seem happy. So, I decide to test my mind powers on her. I'm shocked after hearing what's going on in her head.

Her thoughts were, "OMG. I can't believe she got captain. Lexi does not deserve it at all. But I need to keep smiling or else she's going to act all mad at me for not being happy for her. But seriously, did she like cheat or something because I don't think she has the potential to even be on the team?"

"I never thought I would be saying this to you of all people but, we can't be friends anymore Britney.", I tell her as I walk away. I go to the basketball court to ask Coach for another jacket. I can't keep losing all my friends like this. I thought this power would be cool to have but it seems to have backfired.

I see Coach Harris; he's filling up some new basketballs with air. He notices me and says, "Lexi Fernandez, captain of the 2025-26 girls' basketball team. Hey, what happened?"

I ask him if he has any extra captain's jackets with him but he says no. I told him that I would be completely fine even if he gave me a normal jacket which he gave to the rest of my teammates. He still insists that since I'm captain, I'll wear the captain's jacket and not and ordinary one. He also says that he's run out of all jackets for girls' basketball team.

I sigh thinking that I'll never get rid of the situation this power has gotten me into. I try bargaining with him by asking if I could wear any other jacket which I had at home but he said that all team members have to be in the appropriate sports uniform.

He asks me if anything was troubling me because he has been my P.E. teacher since 6th grade and he has never seen me so worked up about anything. He's known me a long time and there's no fooling him; he can tell when I'm lying. So, I just decide to tell him the truth about how when I wear the jacket and close my eyes, I can read people's minds."

He smiles and tells me to read his thoughts if that is actually true.

His thoughts are, "I give this jacket to all the captains. You are correct, it does give you the opportunity to read people's minds. It can cause good things to happen, for example getting rid of fake friends. However, it can also cause bad things to happen, it could make others' thoughts interfere with your daily life. Now I have given you this jacket with such a power to test your responsibility. Now that you know all this, prove to me that you are worthy of being team captain."

Well at least now I know the base of how this whole thing began. I thank him for sharing with me this information. I leave the basketball court as a wiser and more determined person than when I entered it. All I know is that this power is going to make my life a lot more difficult.

TWENTY

YES GIRL: ONE DAY, ONE WORD

I only wanted my book. That was it. A quick mission: go into my little brother's room, retrieve The Silent Patient, and head back to the comfort of my own bed. Mike had borrowed it last night—probably to impress some girl by pretending he was into psychological thrillers—and I didn't want it turning into one of those "permanently borrowed" sibling items. His door was half-open, sunlight slicing across his floor in angled streaks, and I barged in without knocking, the way siblings do when they're not in the mood to negotiate.

The book was right there on his desk, next to a protein bar he hadn't finished and a pair of socks that looked old enough to be artifacts. I grabbed the novel, made a face, and was about to turn on my heel when he looked up from his phone.

"Hey, Michelle," he said lazily, not even glancing up. "Can you bring me my phone charger from downstairs?"

I blinked. Ordinarily, I would've rolled my eyes and tossed a sarcastic comment over my shoulder. Something like, "Get it yourself, you annoying brat." But instead, without even thinking, I heard myself say, "Sure."

Mike actually looked up, surprised. "Wait. What?"

"Yeah," I said again, shrugging. "I'll get it."

He stared at me like I'd grown a second head. To be honest, I was just as baffled. Why had I said yes? It wasn't some grand gesture. It was just… easier. Simpler. A "yes" that came out before the "ugh" could catch up.

And that—though I didn't know it at the time—was how it started.

By the time I'd found his charger on the kitchen counter and returned it to him, I'd said "yes" three more times. Mom intercepted me in the hallway and asked if I'd help her carry in groceries. I said yes. Dad, who was sitting in the living room with his tablet, waved me over and asked if I had "a sec" to watch a funny dog video. I did. The video was four minutes long and featured a corgi in a tutu, but I nodded and smiled the whole way through.

Then, as I was heading towards the stairs, our neighbour Mrs. Carver knocked on the window and gestured for help with her garden hose. Normally I would've pretended not to see her. But today? You guessed it—I said yes.

There I was, standing outside in fuzzy slippers, untangling a rubber snake that looked like it had been through a war. As I wrestled with the hose, the thought popped into my head, casual and absurd: What if I said yes to everything today? Just for one day. No hesitation. No "maybe laters" or "I'll think about its." Just… yes.

It sounded like something from a self-help book or a cheesy rom-com, but in that moment, I couldn't shake it. My curiosity got the better of me. Could one word actually change the way a day unfolds?

Back inside, my phone buzzed. It was Jess, my best friend and frequent source of chaos. Thrift store run? I need a distraction. Also, I need your opinion on something hideous. I was still wearing pyjama pants and had a muffin in the toaster oven. But the rule had already planted itself. So I replied, Yes.

Two hours later, I was standing in front of a mirror wearing a neon pink jacket that looked like it belonged to a backup dancer from an '80s aerobics video. Jess was howling with laughter.

"You're wearing that," she said between giggles.

"No way," I said.

"You said you were saying yes to everything today."

I looked at myself. The jacket squeaked when I moved. It had padded shoulders. It sparkled. And it was warm—distressingly warm.

"I hate you," I muttered.

Jess raised her eyebrows. "That's not a no."

I sighed. "Fine. Yes."

We wandered through the store for another hour, with me squeaking every time I reached for a hanger. Jess caught on to my yes-rule fast and started testing the boundaries. "Should we buy matching bucket hats?" Yes. "Should we compliment strangers?" Yes. "Should we get a drink from that weird café that only sells lavender-infused stuff?" Yes.

At the café, the barista offered me a "secret menu" drink. I nodded before I could stop myself. What arrived was a hot matcha-lavender-chili monstrosity that smelled like soap and tasted like regret. I drank the whole thing, because when you commit to chaos, you commit hard.

The compliments to strangers were less horrifying, though slightly awkward. I told a woman in a business suit that her walk was "confident in a powerful CEO way." I told an elderly man that his beard made him look like "a wizard with property investments." Most people smiled. One guy blushed. I was kind of impressed with myself.

Then we passed the community center. A hand-painted sign outside read: Open Mic Night – TONIGHT ONLY! All Talents Welcome!

Jess didn't even look at me before pointing. "You're doing that."

"Absolutely not," I said. "You're doing that," she repeated.

I stared at the sign. A younger version of me might have dreamed about something like this—being onstage, doing stand-up or telling stories—but that version got buried under anxiety somewhere in ninth grade. Still, the word hung in the air like a dare.

"Yes," I said, barely believing myself.

The sign-up sheet was a mixture of predictably bizarre entries. One guy had written "DJ Steampunk – Ambient Sound Journey." Another said "Yvonne – Interpretive Yodeling." I scribbled my name next, still unsure of what I'd actually do.

"Stand-up," Jess suggested. "You've got material. Just talk about your day."

So I did. Kind of. I spent the next few hours jotting down bullet points—"weird drink," "wizard beard," "Mrs. Carver and the hose"—while nervously eating chips and listening to Jess hype me up like I was going to the Olympics. I changed nothing about my outfit. If I was going to make a fool of myself, I was going to look like a neon traffic cone doing it.

When they called my name, my heart tried to leap out of my chest. I stepped onto the stage and blinked under the gymnasium lights. People were watching—eating, sipping, smiling. I cleared my throat and launched into the story of my yes-day.

I talked about Mike and the charger, the groceries, the chaos of helping my neighbour with her snake-hose. I told them about the spam call where I said yes and ended up listening to a man named Ray explain solar panels to me while I cleaned the bathroom. I talked about the café drink that tried to assassinate my taste buds, and yes, the jacket. Every time I paused, people laughed—real, unforced laughter that rolled towards me like a wave.

I didn't know it was possible to feel scared and completely alive at the same time, but I did. The nerves were still there, but beneath them was something sharper—joy.

When I stepped offstage, Jess practically tackled me. "You were incredible," she whispered. "Like, you could do this for real."

"Don't get ahead of yourself," I said, grinning like an idiot.

By the time I collapsed into bed that night, I felt like I'd lived five days instead of one. My cheeks ached from smiling. My feet hurt from walking. My brain buzzed with memories, strange and sweet.

Saying yes to everything didn't make me a different person. But it did make me see the day differently. Instead of resisting everything the world threw at me, I leaned in. I let things happen. I invited the weirdness in, and the weirdness brought friends.

Would I do it again? Probably not tomorrow. Or even next week. The exhaustion was real. But something about that day stuck with me—a reminder that comfort zones are just invisible fences we build ourselves. One "yes" at a time, I had climbed out.

And if I'm being honest?

I don't think I'll ever completely go back in.